mona lisa smile

mona lisa smile

A Novel by

Deborah Chiel

Based on the Motion Picture Written by

Lawrence Konner & Mark Rosenthal

AN ONYX BOOK

ONYX
Published by New American Library, a division of
Penguin Group (USA) Inc., 375 Hudson Street,
New York, New York 10014, U.S.A.
Penguin Books Ltd, 80 Strand,
London WC2R 0RL, England
Penguin Books Australia Ltd, 250 Camberwell Road,
Camberwell, Victoria 3124, Australia
Penguin Books Canada Ltd, 10 Alcorn Avenue,
Toronto, Ontario, Canada M4V 3B2
Penguin Books (N.Z.) Ltd, Cnr Rosedale and Airborne Roads,
Albany, Auckland 1310, New Zealand

Penguin Books Ltd, Registered Offices:
80 Strand, London WC2R 0RL, England

Published by Onyx, an imprint of New American Library,
a division of Penguin Group (USA) Inc.

First Printing, November 2003
10 9 8 7 6 5 4 3 2

Printed in the United States of America

For the girls of the Emerson House Pit—
a long time ago

Chapter One

Dusk, the sky a wash of violet, pink, and dark blue. Curled up on her seat next to the window on the Super Chief train out of Los Angeles, Katherine Watson watched the sun slowly dip below the horizon. The last time she had checked with the conductor, they were somewhere in the middle of Nebraska. By tomorrow evening, she would be in Chicago, halfway across the country, halfway to her final destination.

Wellesley, Massachusetts.

Tired as she was from the previous night and the discomfort of trying to sleep sitting up, she felt a jolt of anticipation each time she thought about her soon-to-be new home: Wellesley College. The words alone were enough to make her shiver with excitement. Spoken aloud, they conjured up a rich and rarified universe, so different from UCLA, where she had gotten her B.A. and master's in art history.

The Super Chief train was famous for catering to the whims of Hollywood celebrities, but Katherine, traveling coach class, hadn't yet spotted any actors. Instead of eating in the dining car, where gourmet meals and fine wines were served, she had packed a couple of brown paper bags with ham and cheese sandwiches, potato chips, and oranges.

Katherine couldn't afford to travel first-class, but the scenery was free. She didn't have to pay one penny more to enjoy the same view as the first-class passengers: the arid California desert, the snow-topped Colorado Rockies, the flat wheat fields of Nebraska. A hundred years earlier, her great-grandma Katie—a dark-eyed beauty whose wide mouth, vibrant smile, and name Katherine had inherited—had driven across the continent in a covered wagon. A widow at twenty-seven, Katie had traveled with her three children under the age of ten and five down-filled quilts to keep them warm through the bitter-cold winter months. She had also brought the family Bible, a rifle, and a couple of paintbrushes that belonged to her late husband. She had sold almost everything else to pay for a fresh start out West, where land was available for anyone who was brave or crazy enough to homestead.

Katie had survived life-threatening hail and snowstorms, hostile Indians, and rustlers who had tried to steal her cows. Driven by an iron will and a bold spirit, she had turned her back on the past to build her family a new home and a new life in northwestern Montana. According to family legend, Katherine looked a lot like her great-grandmother; two faded photographs taken when Katie was past fifty lent some truth to this notion.

Katherine had also inherited Katie's restlessness and sense of adventure. She had a good teaching job at Oakland Teachers College and a boyfriend who was crazy about her, but she craved a change. She was excited about introducing her West Coast ideas to Wellesley; she imagined herself throwing open the windows and ridding the classrooms of the stuffy East Coast beliefs about life in general and art in particular.

She was nervous, too. She was the first person in her family to graduate from college, and her background was starkly different from that of the Wellesley students and alumnae. Many of the faculty members were also graduates of Wellesley or one of the other Seven Sister colleges—the elite all-girl equivalents of the Ivy League men's schools that included Yale, Harvard, and Dartmouth. No matter how hard she might try to fit in, she would probably dress and sound like an outsider to these girls, in their little black dresses, the cashmere sweater sets, and pearl necklaces, all calculated to create a casually expensive look. She would never share or desire their haughty sense of entitlement. Katherine reminded herself that she was offered the year-long position because the hiring committee had been impressed by her credentials, not her pedigree.

Wellesley College was where she wanted to be. She was thirty years old and single. Many of her friends from school were married and had a couple of kids. They thought she was nuts for moving east to teach and research her doctoral dissertation.

Women had proven their worth during World War II, taking over the jobs left empty by the men who had gone to be soldiers. Katherine's own mother had worked the night shift at a munitions factory. "I'm making bombs to blow those damn Nazis to hell and back," she liked to boast. She left the house every afternoon at five o'clock with a lunchbox and a kerchief over her head to keep her hair from getting caught in the machinery. The work was tedious and dangerous. "Best job I ever had," she always said. "Goes to show that us girls can do it just as fast and good as the guys."

Then the war ended, the men returned from overseas, and Katherine's mother, along with the other Rosie the Riveters, lost her place on the assembly line. She had no choice but to go back to cleaning rich people's houses, which meant she came home in time for supper but was too tired and cranky to cook. Life went back to normal. The ex-soldiers got all the best jobs, the single women became their secretaries again or took the jobs that the men didn't want, and the married women stayed home, even if they didn't have children.

Katherine didn't want to trade her brand-new career for a more sedate home life. She loved Paul, but she didn't know if she loved him enough to give up the opportunity of teaching art history to college students. A year spent at the opposite end of the continent, among some of the brightest young women in the country was a vastly appealing prospect.

In the meantime, she had the rare treat of time alone with nothing to do but think and read and sketch the changing late-summer landscape. Almost no rain had fallen in Oakland, and the lawns were parched, the hillsides brown and dusty. In the very middle of America, the meadows were green and lush, the trees just starting to show their fall colors.

In Chicago, Katherine boarded the Twentieth-Century Limited, the glamorous star of the New York Central Railroad. A red carpet was rolled out for everyone who boarded the luxurious Limited. And no sitting up overnight: even economy-class passengers had to buy a bed. So Katherine slept in a roomette, the least expensive of the accommodations available for the sixteen-hour trip.

She was exhausted and grateful for any kind of bed after two nights of sitting up on the train, and almost no sleep the night before she had left Los Angeles. She had been jolted awake from a dream that she instantly forgot and squinted at the clock. Two a.m. She patted the space next to her in bed, where Paul should have been, turned over, and found him slouched in the chair they kept meaning to get recovered. He was smoking a cigarette, pretending to be absorbed in a magazine she knew he had already read. He had turned on the small reading lamp, but the almost full moon shining through the window behind him cast enough light to make her feel as if she could see right into his soul.

"What's the matter?" she asked, even though she knew the answer.

They had an agreement. He wouldn't smoke in the bedroom. She wouldn't throw away any of leftovers in the refrigerator, even if they looked like a science project. He took a last puff on the cigarette and stubbed it out. The window was open, but the room smelled of smoke. She knew better than to mention it.

"I couldn't sleep," he said.

"That's a new one." Paul had once slept through an earthquake that had damaged several buildings a couple of miles from his house. "Bad dream?"

"No, it was good," he said. He crossed the small room, sat down next to her on the bed, and took her hand. "We were here. It was tomorrow morning. You had overslept and missed the train to Wellesley."

Katherine's alarm clock was set for six o'clock, and she was all packed. It hadn't taken long. She didn't have many clothes; one entire suitcase was filled with books, photographs, and her art slides.

"Come on." She tried to keep her tone light. They had been arguing all week about her decision to take the job at Wellesley, ever since last Wednesday, when she had received the call from Dr. Staunton, the head of the art department.

The phone had rung at six thirty in the morning, rousing Katherine from a deep sleep. She grabbed the receiver, as she swam up to consciousness with Dr. Edward Staunton's voice greeting her on the other end. With typical Eastern arrogance, he hadn't bothered to remember the three-hour time difference between Massachusetts and California. She was so shocked to hear his voice that the words almost didn't register; for a moment, she wondered if she were dreaming.

Afterward, she tried to recall for Paul exactly what he had said: ". . . rather last minute . . . unavoidable circumstances . . . no reflection on your abilities . . . this late date . . . must have your response posthaste. . . ."

She didn't give him an immediate answer. Paul was lying there next to her, wide-awake, the expression in his eyes as transparent as a clear mountain lake. *Please don't go. Stay here with me.*

"What a jerk," he said. "Snaps his fingers and figures you'll come running."

She didn't want to argue, so she waited until he left for work, then dialed the operator and placed a person-to-person call to Dr. Staunton. Yes, she told him. She would be happy to join his department and teach History of Art 100. And yes, she could arrive in time for the fall semester.

Paul lit up another cigarette, resuming the description of his dream. "You were happy about missing the train. You said, 'They're a bunch of snotty, rich, white spoiled girls. Besides, they just offered me the job. I must have been their last choice.' "

So what? She didn't care that the job was hers by default. What mattered was that she would be teaching at Wellesley.

"Stop it," she said, waving away the smoke.

Paul was always so sure he knew what was right for her. They had met, of all places, at the Griffith Park Zoo, where she had worked part-time as a guide. Paul's two nephews were visiting from San Francisco; the older one, Ethan, knew more than she did about the tropical birds, and Aaron had asked lots of questions about the mating habits of the monkeys and gorillas.

They bumped into each other again at the zoo's cafeteria, where the boys were gorging themselves on hot dogs, French fries, and ice cream. Paul insisted on buying her coffee. By the time the boys had finished their double-scoop chocolate chip cones, she had given him her phone number and agreed to a date, sans monkeys, toucans, and kids.

That was almost two years ago. Although they didn't share an apartment, they spent so much time together that sometimes it did seem silly for them both to pay rent. Still, their bohemian, easygoing relationship suited Katherine just the way it was.

Paul was a lawyer whose clients were itinerant laborers who picked grapes, lettuce, and other farm crops for shamefully low wages. He could outtalk most of his opponents, but he wasn't going to change Katherine's mind about accepting the Wellesley job offer.

"Classes start next week," he reminded her. "It's an insult."

"I'm not insulted."

He stood up and paced the room. "What do you do when you know someone's making a mistake? Do you try to stop them?"

She glared at him. "You mean like the one you're making right now?"

They had been over this same ground again and again. If they weren't debating her future, she might have been amused by his persistence. He was sounding like a petulant little boy bent on eating an ice-cream cone before dinner, even though he'd been told he couldn't have one.

But this *was* about her life, and she wished he could at least try to share her excitement.

"I've never understood this dream you have of teaching at an elitist school like Wellesley," he said, repeating himself for what must have been the hundredth time.

The irony was that Paul's father had graduated from Yale University and his mother from Smith College, another of the Seven Sister schools. Katherine had met his parents only once: Paul's father had driven down to LA for business, and his mother had come along to shop and visit friends. They had gone for dinner at the Bel Air Hotel restaurant, where Paul's mother had drunk three martinis in quick succession.

Katherine had seen Paul make friends with a roomful of strangers. But as soon as he sat down with his parents, he was transformed into a sullen little boy who couldn't stop fidgeting with the silverware. His parents ignored his strange behavior and chatted with Katherine.

Mrs. Moore urged her to order anything she wanted on the menu. ("Sky's the limit, dear. My husband loves spending money on pretty young girls," she said with a mirthless smile.) Once they realized that Katherine didn't know any of their friends in Los Angeles, they stopped including her in their conversation. Katherine didn't much care. The food was delicious; the wine was the best she had ever tasted. But the atmosphere at the table was strained. Katherine had the impression that the potential for an ugly argument lay just below the surface of their polite chitchat.

"That place doesn't stand for anything real," Paul said now. He was staring out the window, his back to her, his shoulders hunched in a gesture of resignation.

"How would you know? The smartest girls in the country go there."

"What makes you think they'll want to learn from someone who never knew her father? Whose mother cleaned homes for a living?"

"Don't talk about my family," she snapped. She didn't want to fight with him, not when they were only hours away from saying goodbye to each other. But some words were too painful to ignore, some boundaries so vulnerable that they had to be defended against all trespassers. Even Paul, the person she loved most in the world.

He glared at her with hurt, angry eyes. "Why not? They'll want to know about your family. All they care about is pedigree."

They? Who were *they*? This was a side of Paul she had never seen before, and it frightened her. Was he talking about the Wellesley faculty and students? Or did he mean his parents, their friends, the people with whom he had grown up?

"Do me a favor," he said, spitting out the words as if he had a bad taste in his mouth. "If you hate the place, don't stay there out of stubbornness. You belong here with me."

No, Paul, she thought, biting back words too wounding to say aloud. *I'm suffocating here. I need to meet other people, explore different ideas.*

A new vista, unfamiliar surroundings would give her a chance to figure out exactly where she did belong.

Katherine changed in New York for the Eastern Seaboard Express, oddly named for a train that seemed to stop in every little coastal town in Connecticut, Rhode Island, and Massachusetts. She sat on the edge of her seat, hot and sweaty from the unseasonable warmth, dressed in a new wool suit she had bought on sale at Neiman-Marcus, a splurge she already regretted.

She was too tired to sketch, too nervous to read, too hot to think about anything except stripping off her clothes and taking her first shower in almost four days. Desperate for relief from the smoky car, the mind-numbing combination of heat and humidity, her anxious thoughts, she closed her eyes and imagined herself walking on the beach at twilight, the cool ocean breeze rustling her hair. Was Paul with her? Or was she alone? She couldn't decide . . . and then the conductor was shaking her awake, telling her they were coming into Wellesley.

The platform was crowded with arriving students. Girls in fashionable suits and dresses. Girls who looked confident and sophisticated, full of laughter and happy anticipation. Girls who didn't look wilted or tired, whose hair was perfectly in place in spite of the heat. They greeted one another gleefully as the porters unloaded heavy trunks from the baggage car. "Muffy! Betty! Dosie! Susan! Bibbie!"

Returning students hugged each other and screamed with excitement. It was the fall of 1953. Russia had the atomic bomb, and America had Senator Joe McCarthy. The country was gripped by paranoia and fear. At Wellesley, where traditions buffered reality, faculty and students watched dispassionately, voyeurs to someone else's drama.

Katherine was instantly transported back to

fourth grade, when she had arrived at a birthday party in her best dress, the one with the crinoline peeking out, and realized that all the other girls had come in shorts and matching halter tops. Why had everyone but she known what to wear? What signals had she missed? She borrowed a pair of shorts from the girl giving the party, which would have been okay, except that Katherine was so skinny that the shorts kept falling down below her waist.

The students were lining up next to at a cab stand. Katherine set her suitcases by the curb and approached a porter, who was hailing a cab. "The bus?" she asked.

He glanced at her and chuckled. "Keep walking," he said.

No buses? She thought about the long walk up the hill to the campus. She was calculating how much money she had to live on until her first paycheck, then started walking.

As she trudged up the hill to the college, she almost had to pinch herself to believe she was here. Wellesley looked like pictures she had seen of the English university towns Cambridge and Oxford, with gracious ivy-covered Georgian-style buildings and a green expanse of carefully manicured lawn intersected by neat little paths bordered by flowers.

Girls rushed past on foot or bicycle. The sun

was shining, and the blue sky could have been lifted from a Canaletto painting. The white clouds drifting overhead were fluffy soft pillows, as in the Constable landscapes she'd always admired.

The hill was even steeper than Katherine had imagined. Maybe it just seemed so because she was carrying suitcases and a winter coat slung over her arm. Halfway up, she wished she had taken a taxi. She stopped to ask a man raking grass how to get to the faculty housing. He gave her directions and a pitying look, but didn't offer to help her with her bags.

Ten minutes later, she reached her new home, a rambling stone building with a wide, welcoming porch. On either side of the front door were oversize cushioned rocking chairs, easily big enough to seat two people.

She found the housing director in her office. "It's a shame you didn't come yesterday," said Mrs. Babcock, a short, gray-haired woman whom Katherine had spoken with by phone after she had accepted Dr. Staunton's job offer. "It's so quiet before the girls arrive."

She handed Katherine a set of keys and led her up a couple flights of stairs to her two-room suite, which was much bigger and better appointed than she had expected. The living room had windows on two sides that faced the leafy green campus. It was furnished with a sofa covered in a muted floral print, an armchair in the same pattern, and a low oak coffee table. There were a tiny, spotless kitchenette and, beyond that, a sun-filled bedroom. The bed was covered with a white chenille spread, and against one wall was an old-fashioned oak rolltop desk, alongside a low wooden bookshelf.

"It's lovely," Katherine said, longing to pull back the bedspread and fall fast asleep.

"Just a few rules," said Mrs. Babcock. "No holes in the walls. No loud noises. No pets. No radios or hi-fis after eight on weekdays, ten on weekends. No hot plates. And no male visitors."

A few rules? Katherine forced herself to keep a straight face. She might as well have arranged to live in a convent, for all the regulations she'd have to follow. Choking back a giggle, she forced herself not to think of how Paul would react to Mrs. Babcock's list of no's. But after living on her own all this time, Katherine couldn't never put up with so many restrictions. This was 1953, not the Victorian Age, and she was too old to be told what to do. She frowned and tried to look properly serious.

"Anything wrong?" Mrs. Babcock asked.

"I'm not sure I can go a whole year without a hot plate," Katherine said.

Mrs. Babcock frowned. Rules were rules. Miss Watson would have to find herself other accommodations. She suggested that Katherine call Nancy Abbey, a faculty member who lived close to campus in her own home. Nancy occasionally rented rooms to female faculty members, she said. Nancy probably wouldn't agree to a hot plate in the room, but she might offer Katherine kitchen privileges.

Katherine thanked Mrs. Babcock and made a quick call to Nancy Abbey. Yes, said Nancy, as it happened, she did have a room available. Why didn't Katherine come right over to take a look at it and have a cup of tea?

Nancy Abbey lived in a large, well-furnished, three-story Victorian house. An attractive girl who appeared to be in her mid-thirties, she was dressed in a fashionably jacketed dress accessorized by a thin pearl choker. Her dark hair was carefully permed, each strand neatly in place, and her glasses hung from a chain around her neck.

When Katherine admitted that she had just arrived in town after a three-day train ride, Nancy quickly put together a plate of sandwiches along with a pot of tea and began fussing over her like a mother hen.

Katherine was more tired than hungry, and she was eager to solve her housing situation. But Nancy seemed so determined to play the hostess that she nibbled on a sandwich and drank two cups of tea. Finally, Nancy decided it was time to show the room. She led Katherine up a curved staircase and threw open a door.

"Don't you just love chintz?" she asked.

Katherine gaped at the explosion of floral patterns that covered every surface of the bedroom that was for rent in Nancy Abbey's home.

"And look." Nancy pulled back the chintz bedspread to reveal a pair of pink floral sheets.

"They match," said Katherine, not knowing what else to say.

Nancy giggled. The lamp next to the bed was also covered in flowered fabric, with a thin ribbon tied in a bow around the middle. "Sweet, right?"

Katherine managed a weak smile. "You decorated the place?"

"Guilty," Nancy said, giggling again as she handed Katherine a key tied to a big red ribbon. "You're here, my room's down the other end, and in between is Amanda Armstrong. You'll meet her later. She's the school nurse." She pursed her lips, as if holding herself back from adding something more about Amanda.

As Katherine followed Nancy down the stairs, she noticed the collection of black-and-white photographs that hung on the wall. Peering closer, she realized that these pictures were of Nancy and her family.

"You grew up here?" she said.

"My whole life. You'll meet my folks when they visit."

"They visit?" It was hard to imagine living in one place her whole life, harder still to think of staying on in that home as an adult.

"Regularly," Nancy said, pushing open a swinging porthole door that led to the kitchen.

Katherine might as well have been talking to a creature from another planet, a place where the customs and traditions were utterly different from anything that was familiar to her. There were so many other questions she wanted to ask, but she held her tongue and simply said, "You teach speech and elocution?"

"And poise. Dinners are communal, so I'll handle that," she said. "But breakfast and lunch you're on your own, so"—she opened the refrigerator door—"we each get our own shelf."

By way of explanation, she pointed to the top shelf, which was labeled AMANDA'S SHELF. The one below had a small sign that read NANCY'S SHELF.

She smiled at Katherine, who wouldn't have known what to say even if Nancy were to stop talking long enough to listen.

"I'll make your label this evening. I don't need to tell you that everything on our individual shelves is sacrosanct."

Katherine nodded. *Sacrosanct. Of course.*

"I just knew when we met we'd be instant friends," said Nancy.

Chapter Two

On the first day of the semester, the weather turned from summer to fall. Katherine woke up shivering. She had left the windows wide-open, and a brisk wind was rustling through the trees. The sky was clear blue, the sun shining, but the temperature had dipped into autumn. Mother Nature knew better than to fool with Wellesley College tradition. And tradition dictated that the girls turn out for classes in their class beanies and newly purchased cashmere sweater sets, plaid skirts, matching knee socks, and saddle shoes.

Tradition also demanded that every member of the Wellesley community attend first-day services at Houghton Memorial Chapel, a Gothic-style church with a soaring spire and two huge Tiffany stained glass windows. The elaborate, decades-old ritual began with the chapel bells issuing a sonorous summons heard in every corner of the campus. Faculty members, Katherine among them, seated themselves on the podium. Other college employees, including secretaries, cooks, maids, and porters, found places at the back of the chapel.

The students streamed out of their residence halls. The earlier arrivals congregated on the spacious chapel steps; those who lagged behind to drink another cup of coffee gathered on the lawn in front of the chapel. Joan Brandwyn the senior class president, ran through the crowd, rushing to get up the front steps before the bells fell silent.

As the choir began to sing "Lift Thine Eyes" by Mendelssohn, Joan caught her breath, straightened her beanie, and approached the chapel door. She knocked loudly four times.

Dr. Jocelyn Carr, president of the college, stood waiting on the other side of the door. "Who knocks on the door of learning?" she demanded.

"I am Every Woman," Joan responded with the customary convocation day response.

"What do you seek?" President Carr, too, followed the prescribed script.

"To awaken my spirit through hard work and dedicate my life to knowledge," replied Joan in a clear, strong voice.

"Then you are welcome. All women who seek to follow you may enter. I now declare the academic year begun!"

President Carr threw open the door. The girls erupted in a thunderous cheer, almost drowning out the Vivaldi. They rushed into the hall as the choir brought the piece to its joyous conclusion. The director raised her baton again. The entire audience stood up to sing the chapel anthem, a glorious rendition of the hymn "O God Our Help in Ages Past."

The academic year of 1953–54 had officially commenced.

Dr. Staunton was a very busy man. He said so himself each time Katherine telephoned his office to let him know she had arrived on campus. After the third call, she gave up trying to schedule a meeting to discuss curriculum. A memo signed by Dr. Staunton's secretary advised her that she was responsible for teaching a section of the History of Art 100 survey course three mornings a week at nine o'clock. Katherine had brought her own set of slides, magazine articles, and provocative pieces from *Art Journal* and *Art News*. Recalling the unpleasant tone of her interview, she decided she would do better if she didn't get into a discussion with her department chairman about what she should—or shouldn't—teach.

The call had finally come from his secretary: Dr. Staunton would see her on Tuesday at ten in the art department conference room.

Bright morning sunshine poured through the stained glass windows as Katherine walked into the room. A table was polished to a dark mahogany brown. Delicate china teacups, each decorated with a different floral pattern, were stacked one inside the other on a large silver tray in the middle of the table, alongside a gleaming silver tea service.

Gracious living. The college catalog had described in loving detail Wellesley's long-standing traditions: Flower Sunday and Hoop-rolling, Stepsinging, and Junior Show; afternoon tea, roast beef, and Yorkshire pudding for Sunday lunch after chapel services, dinner once a week by candlelight.

Katherine's only experience with candlelight dinners had been at the beachfront restaurant where she had waitressed for a couple months after high school. The place served fancy French food, which the staff was not allowed to eat (though they managed to grab their fill of escargot, onion soup, and duck à l'orange when the managers weren't looking). Katherine recalled vividly the faces of the customers—rich, well-groomed, many of them from the Hollywood community—made to look younger and prettier, all the flaws wiped away by the soft glow of the flickering candles.

The people seated around the conference table exuded the scent of entitlement and power. They greeted her cordially but managed to make it clear that she was not one of them, at least not yet.

They were laughing when she walked into the room. Logic told her she was not the butt of their joke. But she had to swallow hard to keep her voice from shaking as the introductions were made. They knew nothing about her life other than the facts listed on her résumé, nothing about where or how she had grown up.

Dr. Carr was the picture of well-preserved elegance in her well-fitted tweed suit and double-strand of large white pearls. "Katherine Ann Watson, magna cum laude, UCLA dean's list, published in the *Art Review*," she said by way of greeting her.

Katherine smiled, sat, and carefully crossed her legs at her ankles. Why, she wondered, did she feel like a naughty girl who'd been summoned to the principal's office?

Dr. Carr gestured to Dr. Staunton: *Your turn.*

Katherine had heard of Dr. Staunton long before she had decided to teach at Wellesley; he was an expert on early Italian masters and had written one of the best-known texts in the field.

"I'm curious about your Ph.D. dissertation topic," said Dr. Staunton.

"Twentieth-century masters," she said.

The small, insular world of art criticism was in a period of transition. *Art News*, *Art Digest*, and *The Nation*, all of which she read as closely as other people read *Life* and *Time*, were abuzz with articles about Jackson Pollock and Willem DeKooning.

The so-called Action Painters were causing a storm of discussion in New York, and in California, Richard Diebenkorn and David Park were creating a West Coast-flavored version of Abstract Expressionism. Clement Greenberg, the most passionate promoter of American Modernism, was stirring up a hornets' nest of criticism because he was so uncompromising in his absolute belief in the importance of postwar American abstract art.

How could anyone who claimed to be seriously interested in art not be excited by the ferment and controversy? The revolution that had begun in nineteenth-century Paris heralded new ways of thinking not only about art, but also about politics, economics, and psychology. Iconography, subject matter, and connoisseurship were all important to the study of art history, but so many other, equally compelling issues could be discerned in the works of Duchamp, Mondrian, Matisse, and Picasso.

The Boston Museum of Fine Arts owned one of Gauguin's masterpieces, "Where Are We From, What Are We, Where Are We Going?"; she had a postcard-sized copy of it taped over her desk. The first time she had seen Picasso's "Les Demoiselles d'Avignon," she had gaped in frank, openmouthed astonishment. How had he developed such a totally radical vision, unlike anything that had previously existed?

This sense of wonderment was what she hoped to convey to her students. She leaned forward, ready to share her enthusiasm with Dr. Staunton and two women in the room.

"The century's barely half over." Dr. Staunton slapped the top of her folder. He pushed it away, as if discarding the remains of an unappetizing dinner. "Who knows which of the moderns is going to endure? But you suggest—and I quote—'Picasso will do for the twentieth century what Michelangelo did for the Renaissance.' Unquote."

She had written that sentence very early on a summer morning, sitting on the tiny porch that abutted her apartment. Looking up from her typewriter, she had seen a cat prowling around the garbage cans behind the garage. The sun was just rising, the air already warm, the haze formed above the city. She had felt a trill of excitement: to be alive at this midcentury point, a witness to the blossoming of the United States as the center of groundbreaking art. Best of all, to be finished, after so much hard work, with her dissertation

Now, read aloud by Dr. Staunton, her conclusion sounded pompous and overblown. Words fueled by too little sleep, too much coffee.

"In terms of influencing movements," she said, trying to recover her composure. Damn it, she should have realized that Staunton, immersed in the Middle Ages, would be an old fuddy-duddy with no taste for modern art. He had known all along that her field of concentration was the twentieth century. If they had wanted yet another scholar of the Italian Baroque, why had they hired her?

"These canvases that they're turning out these days, with paint dribbled and splotched on them"—he smirked at Dr. Carr and Mrs. Warren, the president of the Alumnae Association—"are they as worthy of our attention as Michelangelo's Sistine Chapel?"

They're all worthy of our attention, she wanted to tell him. *We need to pay attention to everything, instead of ignoring whatever is new and different.*

How else do we draw the line between art and kitsch, genius and mediocre, original and derivative?

"I'm not comparing modern art to the Sistine Chapel," she said, hoping she sounded calmer than she felt.

"Good, that's settled," President Carr broke in. "We can all agree on the beauty of the Sistine Chapel. Your tie, on the other hand, Edward . . ."

She smiled at Katherine as Dr. Staunton glanced down at his tie and nervously fingered the knot. "Mrs. Warren?"

Mrs. Lucinda Warren, a stern-faced woman in her early fifties, wore a small hat, discreetly perched atop her heavily lacquered hair, and white gloves, which she had peeled off with a dramatic flourish. The smoke from her cigarettes swathed her like a veil. She shook her head, no questions.

"Have you ever seen the Sistine Chapel, Miss Watson, actually stood there?" Dr. Staunton continued his interrogation.

He glared at her, as if daring her to answer in the affirmative.

"I've never been to Europe," she said flatly. Although if she had a dollar for every time she had imagined herself there, she could have traveled there and back with first-class accommodations. She had poured over magazines and books, studied the photographs of the most famous cities, museums, cathedrals, memorized the descriptions: France, Italy, Spain . . . Paris, Rome, Florence, Barcelona . . . the Louvre and the Prado. Her dreams were haunted by images of places and masterpieces she had not yet seen.

"Well, I have." Dr. Staunton's voice boomed out, as if addressing a large crowd from a podium. "I've stood there for hours. And there isn't a day that goes by that I don't think about it, that it doesn't fill me with wonder. Do you think Picasso's work has the same impact?"

The pompous fool. Her appreciation for Picasso in no way diminished Michelangelo's genius or devalued the Sistine Chapel as an inspired triumph of human artistic achievement. But Michelangelo was long dead, and people like Dr. Staunton, fearful of change or progress, were obviously threatened by Picasso's redefinition of artistic perspective and continuously evolving vision.

Katherine met Dr. Staunton's gaze and smiled demurely. "Dr. Staunton, I have no problem teaching the core curriculum."

He stared at her above the rims of his bifocals, as if assessing the truth of her statement. "Prehistory to Greece," he said, slapping a bulging file of mimeographed papers onto the desk in front of her. He handed her another file. "Early Renaissance to Romantic. The entire syllabus."

He grunted with the effort of lifting a heavy wooden slide box onto the desk, next to the file folder. "Here are the slides. The numbers correspond with citations in the lectures."

She was beginning to get the picture. And it didn't include Matisse, Monet, and definitely not Picasso. "Oh, I brought my own slides," she said.

He pushed the slide box toward her. "I'm certain you did," he said.

Katherine suddenly felt so tired that all she wanted was to curl up in her chair and fall asleep like a cat in the noonday sun. She rarely took naps. Now she was experiencing an overwhelming, deep-in-the-bones exhaustion that no amount of coffee could overcome.

She forced herself to walk around the table and shake their hands. Her mother had drummed into her the importance of good manners. "Just because we don't have money doesn't mean we don't know how to behave," she would say, reminding Katherine to use "please" and "thank you," and to look people straight in the eye when she was introduced.

"Thank you, Miss Watson, and good luck," said President Carr.

Class dismissed.

Chapter Three

Katherine poured what was left of the coffee into the sink. The coffee was only making a bad case of nerves worse. She'd had trouble sleeping, whether because of excitement or tension she wasn't sure. She had laid her clothes out the night before—the suit from Neiman Marcus and a strand of pearls. This morning, she thought the outfit was too ostentatious, as if she were trying too hard to make the right impression.

She changed into a more casual cotton sweater and navy skirt. When she inspected herself in the mirror, she decided she looked young and inexperienced. She changed back into the suit and drank her coffee. And now, if she didn't hurry up, she was going to be late for her first day of school.

* * *

One of Katherine's roommates Amanda Armstrong—a thin, elegant school nurse in her mid-forties—had accompanied her to class. Just before Katherine walked inside, Amanda said, "Be careful. They can smell fear."

Just what Katherine needed to hear.

The first thing Katherine discovered was that, whether the lecture hall was at Wellesley or at Oakland Teacher's College, it was a big, drab place with bad acoustics and an echo. And that her students were punctual. They were already seated when she hurried into the room.

"Good morning," she said, the words coming out in a breathless rush.

She glanced at the fifty or so girls scattered about the hall and considered asking them all to come sit up front, but thought better of the idea. She remembered Amanda's warning: *They can smell fear.* Her heart was pounding. Any closer, and they would probably hear the pounding, see her terror. She carefully arranged Dr. Staunton's syllabus in front of her.

"This is History of Art," she said, wishing her voice didn't sound so shaky. She took a deep breath and tried to be calm. "We'll be following Dr. Staunton's syllabus."

Her mind was suddenly blank. She couldn't remember what else she was supposed to say or do. The girls were staring at her, their eyes like X rays seeing through her facade to her panic. She'd never been this scared before in front of a class, not even the very first time she had entered a room as the teacher, the person in charge.

She couldn't just stand before them, trying to think of what should come next. She had to do *something*. "What am I leaving out?" she said. Did the question sound as stupid to them as it did to her?

The answer came from a stocky girl in the second row. She had an impish gleam in her eyes and a head of tight brown curls. "Your name."

Her name. How could she have forgotten to introduce herself? She was tempted to walk out of the room and head straight for the train station.

Fighting the impulse, she said instead, "Why don't you go first?"

"Connie Baker," said the stocky girl.

She parted her lips in what she hoped was a smile. "Katherine Watson. Nice to meet you."

"Dr. Watson, I presume?" asked a tall, dark-haired beauty.

Katherine ignored her students' laughter and addressed the girl, whose face was dominated by huge brown eyes that glittered with intelligence. "Not yet. And you are?"

"Giselle Levy." The girl stood up and bowed. Tall and dark haired, she had a face dominated by huge brown eyes that glinted with intelligence.

"All right then," said Katherine, feeling positively dowdy next to Giselle Levy's sultry sophistication. "Can someone get the—"

A pretty redheaded girl in the front rushed to adjust the switch.

"—lights?" said Katherine, as the room went dark. "Thank you, Miss . . ."

"Susan Delacorte," said a voice in the front row.

Slide number one from Dr. Staunton's box: a cave painting of a wounded bison. Katherine stared at the image. There were so many other, more thought-provoking ways to explore the evolution of art and its relevance to twentieth-century culture. Cave paintings established that even primitive man felt compelled to create painted images. But why not establish the link between the important movements of the twentieth-century art world and how they evolved from, or were a reaction to, earlier influences?

Too radical. Instead of raising that question for discussion, Katherine dutifully followed the script set forth by Dr. Staunton. "From the beginning, man has always had the impulse to create art. Anyone know what this is?"

Somebody snorted audibly. If pressed, Katherine would have guessed that that somebody might be named Warren.

"*Wounded Bison,* Altamira, Spain, about 15,000 B.C.," came a more polite response. "Joan Brandwyn," a pretty blond girl identified herself.

"Very good, Joan." Katherine tried to sound less bored than she herself felt about the lecture. "Despite how old these paintings are, they are technically very sophisticated because—"

"Of the shading, the thickness of the line as it moves over the hump of the bison," Joan said, neatly completing her sentence. "Is that right, Miss Watson?"

Katherine nodded. "That's exactly right, yes." She moved to the next slide. "*Herd of Horses.* This is one you are probably less familiar with. It was discovered by archeologists in—"

"1879." A different voice, not Joan's, correctly supplied the information. "Lascaux, France, dates back to 10,000 B.C. Singled out because of the flowing lines depicting the movement of the animal."

"Impressive," said Katherine. "Name?"

"*Herd of Horses.*" Left unsaid was: Don't you remember that you already told us that?

"I meant your name." Katherine decided to ignore her instead of making a fuss about her disrespectful sarcasm.

"We call her Flicka," Giselle Levy yelled.

A dumb joke, but the girls responded with appreciative laughter. *My Friend Flicka* had come out about ten years ago, when these girls were just the right age to go nuts over a movie in which a horse played the starring role.

"I'm Elizabeth Warren. People call me Betty."

Bingo. Just as she'd guessed. Mrs. Warren's daughter. What lousy luck to have the girl turn up in her class. Katherine took a deep breath, then forced a smile that was more for her sake than that of her students because the room was too dark for the girls to see her expression.

"Good," she said. "Betty is also correct. Just because something is ancient doesn't mean it's primitive. For example"—she pulled up the next slide—"*Mycerinus and His Queen.* 2470 B.C. It's a funerary statue of the pharaoh and his queen originally intended to preserve the pharaoh's ka." She translated the word for them. "Soul."

"Made with particularly dense stone, to suggest the permanence and immortality of the soul itself," Connie said.

The comment was so accurate that Katherine wondered whether the girl had memorized the textbook. In fact, all the girls who had spoken up had the information down pat. She was struck by a strange idea. "Have any of you taken art history before?"

The girls responded with a chorus of nos.

"Let's go on," she said, bewildered by the extent of their knowledge. Why take the course if they were already totally familiar with the subject?

She ran through the rest of the slides. Each time an image appeared on the screen, one or more of the girls would instantly call out its name and dates.

Ka-chung went the slide projector: "*Peasant Couple Plowing,* Egypt, sixteenth century B.C."

Next slide: "*Snake Goddess,* Crete, 1600 B.C."

And the one after that: "*Funeral Mask,* Mycenae, 1500 B.C."

Not a moment's hesitation. They had the information down cold.

"Can someone turn on the lights please? Thank you." They were already gathering up their notebooks and bags, getting ready to move on to the next class. But she wasn't about to let them go so easily, not when she was feeling utterly superfluous.

"By a show of hands only," she said, "how many have read the entire text?"

Every hand in the room shot up.

"And the suggested supplements," Susan said.

Then why on earth was she here? Why had Staunton bothered to hire her? He had to know that they had already memorized the entire course. Why bother to show up?

"It's a long way from Oakland State, isn't it?" said Giselle Levy.

Katherine felt her head spinning, as if she might faint. She put a hand on the lectern to steady herself and stared at the girls. Their faces were a blur, and she couldn't remember any of their names.

"My, you do prepare," she said weakly.

Betty stood up and waved her hand. "If you have nothing else for us, we could go to independent study," she said.

Not trusting herself to speak, Katherine shook her head. She began stuffing her lecture notes into her briefcase, wishing the girls would leave quickly so that she could sit down and collect herself.

They were starting to file out when she looked up and noticed Dr. Staunton slipping out the door. How long had he been in the room, and how much had he heard of her exchange with the students? Was he going to make a habit of slinking in to spy on her? If so, she might need a return ticket to California much sooner than she had imagined.

She was homesick. There was no other way to understand what she was feeling. Lonely, miserable, aching to curl up Paul's arms, listening to one of their favorite albums on the record player. She had turned on the radio and happened upon Nat King Cole, but it hurt too much to hear "I've Got a Crush on You" while she was sitting there alone, with Paul three thousand miles away.

She tried to distract herself by unpacking the rest of her books, a tiny painting of the Golden Gate Bridge that Paul had given her as a going-away present, seashells she had collected at Stinson Beach. And her favorite picture of her mother dressed in shorts, lying on the grass at Golden Gate Park, laughing at the camera.

All these mementos of home sharpened the ache in her chest. She thought about going down to the kitchen to make a cup of tea. Then she remembered she had run out of milk, and she would have to borrow some. But Amanda had gone out, and the prospect of a lecture from Nancy about keeping her refrigerator shelf well stocked was too painful to contemplate.

She wasn't sleepy, and she had already prepared her next two lectures. Much as she hated to admit it, she could think of only one thing that might distract her, maybe even cheer her up. She put on her robe and slippers and padded downstairs to use the telephone she shared with her housemates.

She dialed the long-distance operator, asked to place a collect call to Paul's number, and prayed he would be home.

He picked up the phone on the second ring.

"Hello?" The connection was as clear as if he were just down the block.

"It's me," she said quickly, before the operator had a chance to speak.

"Hey!" He sounded surprised. And happy.

She had been scared that he might be upset with her because of their fight on her last night at home—except that, after they had run out of angry words, they had somehow found their way back into each other's arms and silently made love. He was still sleeping when she got up a few hours later, and she didn't want to wake him. So she had kissed him very gently on the cheek and tiptoed out of the house. They hadn't talked since, and she wasn't sure he would want to hear from her anytime soon. She should have known better.

"Collect call from Katherine Watson," said the operator. "Will you accept?"

"Yes, sure," he said, and Katherine's eyes brimmed over with tears. "Everything okay?"

She bit down hard on her lower lip. She was afraid that, if she let herself cry, she might not be able to stop.

"Katherine?" He sounded as if he wasn't sure she was still there.

She swallowed hard, trying to push down the sobs, which felt like large, painful knots in her throat.

"What?" she said, hardly able to speak above a whisper.

"You're having a hard time?" He sounded sad, not pleased to have been proven right.

"Yeah." She felt the weight of his love pressing into her heart, propping up her sagging faith in herself.

"How are the classes?"

Nancy came down the stairs and went into the den. Katherine waited for her to turn on the television, but heard no sound except for her own breath. She felt Nancy's presence just on the other side of the wall, sensed her curiosity.

"Snobs, right?" Paul said. "I don't want to say I told you so."

"You don't have to," Katherine whispered.

"I can't hear you, honey," said Paul.

Nancy had turned on the TV. The jingle for the Marlboro Man commercial was playing.

Katherine raised her voice slightly and pressed the receiver against her mouth. "It's hard to talk."

"Come home," Paul said, his voice thick with longing.

"I'll write you tonight," she promised.

She hung up without saying good-bye, without hearing him say he loved her. She stood by the phone, not moving. She had no idea why she was staying; she only knew that she wasn't going home, at least not anytime soon.

Her reverie was interrupted by Nancy, who called out to her above the noise from the TV, "Were you talking to your fellow?"

Katherine came into the den, which was decorated in reproductions of Early American furniture from Ethan Allen. "He's there. I'm here. Who knows?"

"Long distance is torture," Nancy said sympathetically. "I know. When Lenny left for the South Pacific, it broke my heart. We wrote every day until . . ." Her voice trailed off. She dabbed her eyes with an embroidered linen handkerchief. "He was a great man."

"I'm sorry," said Katherine.

Nancy smiled wanly. "It's a hundred years ago. I'm babbling. Sit down." The sofa fabric matched the Early American decor of the room; the pattern showed a log cabin interior, complete with a tiny hearth and a miniature rocking chair. "It's a convertible, opens to a bed. Isn't that smart?"

The *I Love Lucy* theme came on at the end of the show. Nancy leaned over and turned down the volume on the TV. "I love Lucy, even if she is a Communist," she said.

Katherine had never heard that rumor before. She was about to tell Nancy she must be mistaken when Amanda walked into the room.

"The only thing red about Lucy is her hair," Amanda declared. "And even that's fake. Desi said it, Winchell wrote it." She grinned at Katherine. "I see you survived."

"Barely." But talking to Paul had helped, as did the simple pleasure of watching television with her new friends.

"How about a little dinner now that *Lucy* is over?" said Nancy.

Amanda winked at Katherine behind Nancy's back. "How about a little drink?"

Katherine nodded yes to both suggestions. Suddenly hungry, she followed Nancy into the kitchen, while Amanda went to get wineglasses from the oak breakfront.

"Her companion died in May," whispered Nancy, stirring a pot on the stove.

"Companion?" Katherine took a white linen cloth from the drawer and shook it out onto the table.

" 'Companion,' " Nancy said, still whispering. "Josephine Burns. She taught biology here for thirty years."

Katherine was still puzzling over Nancy's comment when Amanda walked into the kitchen. "Nothing attracts attention more than a whisper," Amanda said, glaring at Nancy. She held up a bottle of red wine and said to Katherine, "I hope you like red."

Katherine drank wine only occasionally, when she and Paul had dinner at a little Italian restaurant in Long Beach where the food was heavily infused with garlic and the squat bottles of Chianti were wrapped in woven straw. French wine was a new experience, one of many this week. She watched Amanda pour the wine into long-stemmed crystal goblets. Were they Nancy's, part of the trousseau she had planned to share with her fiancé? The rims were engraved with a delicate border of tiny grape leaves. They were so much more in keeping with Nancy's girlishly romantic style than Amanda's, which tended to be modern, clean, unfussy.

Looking at Amanda, Katherine realized what Nancy meant by companion: Josephine Burns had been Amanda's "special friend," like the two ladies, both schoolteachers, who had shared a house on her block when she was growing up. Neither had ever been married, and they were totally devoted to each other. "Like two love-birds," her mother often described them, which had confused Katherine until she was older and more sophisticated about the many varieties of human relationships.

The wine was drier than she was used to, but it tasted delicious. As the flush of alcohol spread through her veins, her arms and legs went slightly numb, an odd but not unpleasant sensation. Her doubts fell away. Beginnings were always difficult. But she was an experienced teacher, tough when she needed to be. She could handle Dr. Staunton and her students. With any luck, she could get them all to appreciate that the history of art didn't end with the Renaissance.

Nancy turned on the radio. Patti Page was singing "How Much Is That Doggie in the Window?" Amanda and Nancy joined in the chorus, doing a credible imitation of a barking dog. Katherine took another sip of wine, and then she started barking, too, and giggling because she loved feeling so silly and carefree.

Amanda peeked into the pot. "What are we having?"

"Braised beef and peas." Nancy ladled generous portions of both onto a platter.

"What do you think of our Wellesley girls, Katherine?" Amanda asked.

"They're smart." She groped for the back of her chair and sat down, dizzy from the combination of wine and laughter. Then she admitted, "I'm beginning to wonder what I can teach them."

"Cloth napkins or paper?" Amanda asked Nancy.

"Paper," Nancy said, then changed her mind. "No, cloth. It's an occasion."

Amanda took plates out of the cupboard and handed them to Katherine.

"They're so delicate," Katherine said, setting three places.

Nancy brought the food to the table. "They're Spode. Dreamy, right? I'm registering for the whole collection."

"You're getting married?" Katherine said. She tried to remember Nancy's story about her fiancé. Didn't she say he had died? Or maybe she had a new beau.

She glanced at Amanda, who raised an eyebrow, as if to say: Don't ask me.

"A girl has to be prepared," Nancy said coyly. She seated herself at the head of the table. "Shall we?"

Amanda had decanted the wine into a crystal carafe, which she had brought to the table. Now she refilled her glass and quickly downed most of the contents in one long gulp.

Nancy unfolded her napkin onto her lap. "You'll love it here," she said.

"I already do," said Katherine, almost convinced that she was telling the truth. "Wellesley is beautiful."

Amanda raised the decanter in her direction. Katherine nodded. She really was very lucky: a great place to live, two terrific housemates, and of course, Paul.

Both Amanda and Nancy had lost the people they loved, with whom they were supposed to spend the rest of their lives. How awful for them. She smiled happily and raised her glass in a tribute to them. "It's perfect," she said.

Nancy responded with a smile and a mock half curtsy.

"Don't fool yourself," said Amanda, refilling her glass yet again. "They have claws under those white gloves."

"Who?" she said, stunned by Amanda's sudden mood change.

"The alumnae. Their offspring. The faculty. You name it," Amanda said. She shook a warning finger at Katherine. "Watch out for yourself. Too much independence frightens them."

"Stop it, Amanda!" Nancy admonished.

Amanda brushed her off with a sloppy wave and turned back to Katherine. "Word of advice," she said, slurring the syllables. "Don't let them know they got to you."

"They didn't," Katherine said. She heard the uncertainty in her voice. She hoped Amanda and Nancy didn't.

"Good girl!" said Amanda. She emptied what was left of the wine into her glass. "You almost convinced me."

Katherine brought her own set of slides to the next class. She didn't bother taking attendance, dispensed with formalities, got right down to the business of establishing her authority.

She got to the hall ten minutes early and checked her watch. On the dot of nine, she turned off the lights and jumped right into her lecture. "Last week I saw how well you memorized. Now I'd like to see how well you think."

She pushed the START button on the projector and brought the first slide up onto the screen.

She got the reaction she had expected: squeals of revulsion and lots of nervous titters. No doubt it was the girls' first exposure to a picture of a bloody side of beef hanging from a hook.

"What is that?" Betty said.

"You tell me," said Katherine, managing to conceal her amusement.

"Meat." Connie's statement of the obvious brought peals of laughter from her classmates.

"*Carcass* by Soutine," Katherine said. "1925."

Another predictable response, this one from Susan. "It's not on the syllabus."

"No, it's not," Katherine said agreeably. She waited a beat, allowing time for other comments, but all she got was shocked silence. Wellesley must have its own set of commandments, she thought. One being: "Thou shalt not stray from the syllabus."

"Is it any good?" She strolled up and down the aisle, studying their faces, prodding them to wake up and use their brains. "Come on, ladies.

There is no wrong answer here, no textbook telling you what to think."

Illuminated by the light from the projector, the girls' shadowed faces looked sullen. And fearful, too. Or did Katherine only imagine that they were scared by the challenge of thinking for themselves, without a formula to follow?

"Not so easy, is it?" She almost felt sorry for them. They were some of the brightest girls in the country. Except for a tiny percentage of scholarship students, they came from prosperous, privileged circumstances. Yet they were behaving like a flock of nervous, clucking chickens, their feathers ruffled by the threat of an intruder. Okay, she was willing to play the fox in their midst. Because no matter how tasty the feed or how tidy the coop, most chickens were destined for the roasting pan. Her plan was to show them not only how to evade the fox, but also how to escape their fate.

Not surprisingly, it was Betty who rose to the test. "All right," she said. "It's not good. In fact, I wouldn't even call it art. It's grotesque."

Connie's hand immediately shot up. "Is there a rule against art being grotesque?" she shouted.

"I think there's something aggressive about it," Giselle broke in. "And let's not forget that aggression can be erotic."

Betty snorted. "To you, everything is erotic."

"Everything *is* erotic," Giselle calmly agreed.

A burst of applause and laughter greeted her comeback. Giselle stood up and took a deep bow, playing her part to the hilt.

"But aren't there standards?" asked Susan, sounding genuinely puzzled.

"Of course, there are," Betty declared. "Otherwise, a tacky velvet painting could be equated to a Rembrandt."

"My uncle Ferdie has two tacky velvet paintings. He loves those clowns," said Connie.

Another outburst of laughter. Katherine waited for the room to get calm, then turned to Betty. "Are they art?"

Betty shook her head. "His clowns? No, I don't think we'll be seeing them in any museums."

Katherine had hoped to expand the narrow lens through which her students viewed the world. She would have never guessed that one brief glimpse of a painting by Chaim Soutine could get them to think—and argue—like art critics.

"So that's the defining factor of art: whether a work is considered worthy of being shown in a museum?"

"One of them, yes," Betty said grudgingly. An experienced golfer, she knew when she was headed for a sand trap—and when it was probably too late to salvage her shot.

"She's gonna get you," Giselle sang out. She grinned at Connie. "Watch this. Where does that painting hang, Miss Watson?"

"The Museum of Modern Art, New York City," Katherine said.

Betty glared at Giselle, who played the moment to the hilt with yet another deeply exaggerated bow.

Joan's brow was puckered with confusion. She waved to get Katherine's attention and said, "So if *anything* can be considered art—"

"—Which I'd argue," Betty broke in.

Susan nodded her head. "Me, too."

"Then what's the definition of good art?" Joan said.

Katherine was starting to sort them out as individuals, with strengths and weaknesses and quirks: Joan, so curious and eager to absorb information; Betty, whose aura of self-confidence was tinted with anger; Giselle, sophisticated and slightly exotic; Connie, the cellist who loved to play the clown; and Susan, tentative and unsure of her place in the group.

"Maybe there is none," Connie said.

Betty stared defiantly at Katherine. "It's all a pile of crap."

"I'm offended, Miss Watson," Giselle said facetiously.

"I'm sorry," Betty said, going for the bait like a hungry fish on a juicy worm. "But that can't be considered art. There are standards of technique, composition, color, even subject. So if you're suggesting that that rotted side of meat is art, much less good art, then what are we going to learn?"

Katherine hid a smile. A favorite professor at UCLA had told her that few things were more rewarding to a teacher than an irate student. "If they get angry, you know they're paying attention. You want them to learn, but first, you want them to listen."

"Thank you, Betty. You've just outlined our syllabus," Katherine said. "What is art? What makes it good or bad and who decides? Now anyone not interested can still drop this class without penalty."

The girls looked at her, then at one another. Katherine was close enough to her own college experience that she could guess that they must be wondering if a new teacher plus a new syllabus added up to an easy A. Or was she robbing them of a guaranteed gut course?

She waited. Five minutes passed. Eight or nine girls stood up, some individually, others in pairs, and left the room. Betty Warren stayed in her seat.

Katherine gave her another thirty seconds to gather up her belongings. But Betty didn't move. Katherine was surprised. *Just as well,* she thought. Having Mrs. Warren's daughter in her class meant she didn't have to wonder how or when Dr. Staunton and President Carr would hear about her overhaul of the curriculum.

"Good," Katherine said. Looking up, she noticed that many of the girls were sitting forward in their chairs, as if they didn't know what might happen next. Well, she was not about to disappoint them.

"Here we go." She clicked the FORWARD button on the slide carousel. The image of Soutine's bloodied carcass was replaced by a primitive rendering of a cow standing in a field, lit by a colorful sunset.

"Twenty-five years ago someone thought this was brilliant," Katherine said.

"I can see that," said Connie.

Katherine kept a straight face, revealing nothing.

"Who?" asked Betty.

"My mother," said Katherine. "I painted it for her birthday."

The girls giggled, and someone tossed a balled-up piece of notebook paper at Connie. She shrugged. The joke was on her, but she could take it.

Click. Another image. This one was a black-and-white photograph of a woman. It was a beautiful portrait of a stately woman who was past her prime. But her huge eyes and full lips held a smile, creating a pentimento that more than hinted at the robust beauty she once was.

"That's my mother," Katherine said.

The murmurs that followed her announcement had the timing of a well-rehearsed chorus. Katherine had thought long and hard about whether to show her mother's picture to her students. She had removed it twice from the carousel, then put back the slide at the very last minute. An inner voice had demanded that the photo be included. Thank you, Mama, she wordlessly addressed the image on the screen. You knew I needed you here with me today.

The room was now hushed. Then Susan timidly raised her hand. "It's a snapshot," she said.

"If I told you Ansel Adams had taken it, would that make a difference?" asked Katherine.

"Art isn't art until someone says it is," Betty said loudly.

Katherine nodded. "It's art!" she declared.

Betty rolled her eyes. "The right people," she said, making clear that *she* was one of those right people.

"Who are they?" Katherine said.

"Betty Warren!" Giselle pointed at her classmate. "Aren't we lucky to have one of them right here?"

"Screw you," Betty said under her breath.

Ready for battle, Giselle tapped Betty on the shoulder. "Pardon me?"

Katherine had hoped for a lively debate, not an all-out war. "Think, ladies," she said. Her mother's image disappeared, replaced by the Soutine. The unusual juxtaposition had shaken the girls from their complacency.

She lowered her voice, an educator's trick that drew them into her circle and forced them to pay closer attention. "Soutine looked at this lowly subject matter and transformed it into his own vision of art. Look again, beyond the image. Be open to a different idea."

Most of them were madly scribbling notes. Record your own thoughts, not mine, Katherine wanted to tell them. Maybe that would be next week's lesson.

"Now back to chapter three," she said aloud. "Anyone read it?"

Every hand in the room shot up.

"Oh, Christ," she muttered. They were incorrigible.

Chapter Four

The only reason Joan was late was because she and Tommy had fallen asleep at the frat house. The craziest part was that they hadn't been fooling around, not even necking. She was helping him with his English paper; then they went to the frat for a beer with a couple of his buddies, and she lay down on a sofa, just to take a quick nap. The next thing she knew, Tommy was shaking her awake, telling her to hurry up because it was almost nine thirty.

Curfew on a weeknight was ten o'clock, and the drive from Cambridge to Wellesley took forty minutes. She was the senior class president. She was supposed to set an example, for pity's sake. As Tommy raced down Route 9, Joan closed her eyes, held tight to her seat, and prayed that she'd get back on time—and in one piece.

Mrs. Morgan, her housemother, was standing at the front door, her keys in hand, when Tommy screeched to a stop in front of the residence hall. Instead of waiting for Tommy to come around and open the door for her, she jumped out of the car, sprinted up the sidewalk, and all but threw herself to the ground in front of Mrs. Morgan.

"I know. I'm past curfew," she said breathlessly.

With any luck, the housemother would excuse her this one time because her record was close to spotless. Mrs. Morgan frowned, and Joan's heart sank. "Abject pleading, apologies, forgiveness," she babbled, figuring that a combination of humor and groveling would do the trick.

By now, Tommy had joined her on the steps of the dorm. "Is she giving you any trouble?" he said to Mrs. Morgan.

Tommy was adorable, charming, a shameless flirt. His impish smile could melt the coldest heart, and Joan was totally gone on him. But Mrs. Morgan was a stickler. Joan covered Tommy's mouth with her hand to shut him up, but there was no stopping him.

"If these girls can't get back in time, I say lock

'em out," he said, batting his long eyelashes at Mrs. Morgan.

Mrs. Morgan winked at Tommy. "I'm locking the door," she said. But first, she stepped aside and let Joan pass.

He couldn't stop himself. He had to have the final word. "Keep your eye on that one," he said. "She's very strong willed."

Betty kept promising her mother she would work on the seating charts for her wedding reception, but it was the beginning of October, and she still hadn't given much thought to who would sit where. It was so unutterably *boring*! Her mother said figuring out the seating charts was good training for married life because putting the right people together was key. *For Spencer's sake,* her mother said. When she put it that way, what choice did Betty have?

She changed into her pajamas and robe, stacked the record player with a bunch of her favorite LPs, and spread her wedding notes on the floor of the common room. Pretty soon, Connie showed up with her cello, either to keep Betty company or annoy her, maybe both.

Doris Day was singing "Secret Love," but that didn't stop Connie from reading aloud an advertisement in *The Daily Wellesley*.

" 'When your courses are set, and a dream boat you've met, have a real cigarette. Have a Camel!' "

She drew the bow across the strings of her cello with a dramatic flourish and said, "I have my Camel. I have my courses. Where the hell is my dream boat?"

"Isn't Betty's cousin good enough?" asked Giselle, who strolled into the room in time to hear the end of her question.

"I haven't met him yet."

Betty looked up from her chart and frowned. "Don't encourage her. He's only escorting Connie as a favor."

Connie made a face. *Some friend!* She bowed the cello again, producing a raucous response to Betty's catty remark.

"I didn't mean it that way," Betty backtracked. The words had just popped out of her mouth. She sighed deeply. "I'm under such pressure with this wedding. Do you realize November second is only three weeks from now?"

"Oh, honey." Connie threw her a sympathetic glance. All was forgiven.

"Don't have it," said Giselle. She threw herself into a chair and lit a cigarette.

"Don't come." Betty glared at her. "I'm working on table seating now, so I can just erase your name."

Her curiosity piqued, Giselle pushed herself up and peered over Betty's shoulder. "Let's have a look."

"You just want to see where Bill Dunbar is sitting," Betty said, covering up the paper.

Connie made a face. "No, she doesn't. That's over, right?" she asked Giselle.

Giselle inhaled, pursed her lips, and blew a perfectly formed smoke ring.

Betty and Giselle had been roommates during their freshman year, which was probably the only reason they had become friends. The few times Betty stayed with Giselle in New York, she hadn't felt altogether comfortable. Her parents were divorced, and Giselle lived with her mother on Park Avenue in a stunning two-story apartment. Mrs. Levy was always very nice to her, but she and her friends were so . . . different. They talked a lot, and loudly, about politics and theater. Giselle had told her that her father, who did something on Wall Street, sometimes invested in Broadway plays, which was why Mrs. Levy had a caricature of Ethel Merman hanging in their hallway.

Betty was horrified when Giselle had started dating Bill Dunbar last spring. Everyone knew he was just using her for the s-e-x. But Giselle refused to take Betty's advice to stop seeing him. Was it over between them?

"Clearly," Betty said. As in clearly *not*.

Giselle shrugged. She didn't give a damn what stick-in-the-mud Betty thought. She was still a virgin and about to marry the biggest jerk at Harvard Law. Everyone but Betty knew that the only reason Spencer Jones had gotten into Harvard was because his father, grandfather, and great-grandfather were all alumni.

Giselle struck a pose in the mirror over the mantel. "Do I look like her?" she asked.

"Who?" said Connie.

"Katherine Watson."

Betty smirked. "You mean, Katherine 'Crap Is Art' Watson?"

"I think she's fabulous," Giselle said. She was fascinated with their art teacher, the way she talked and dressed, the fact that she was thirty years old and still single.

Betty, too, found Katherine Watson intriguing, much the way people couldn't stop staring at a sideshow freak or a highway accident. "No man wanted her," she said.

"She's not dead," Giselle shot back.

"She's at least thirty," said Betty, who couldn't imagine turning twenty-five without at least being engaged.

"I guess she never wanted children," mused Connie, who was secretly horrified by the idea of pregnancy and childbirth.

"For your information, Katherine Watson had to take this job to escape California," Giselle said.

"That's ridiculous!" said Betty, who had taken Psychology 101 in her sophomore year and studied Carl Jung. She had decided then that Giselle made up extravagant stories as a way to get attention.

"She had a torrid affair with a Hollywood movie star. She came here to get away," said Giselle.

"Please." Betty rolled her eyes.

The thing about Giselle was that, every once in a while, what everyone thought was a crazy, made-up story turned out to be the truth. But because Giselle was such a convincing liar, the girls could never be sure until they picked up *Life* or *Look* or one of the screen magazines, and the rumor turned out to be fact.

"Who was it?" Connie said.

Giselle smiled.

"Don't be a pimple," Connie pleaded. "Tell."

"William Holden," said Giselle.

"Fantastic!" Connie exclaimed.

"I don't believe any of this," Betty said with a sneer.

"Women like Katherine don't get married because they *choose* not to," said Giselle.

"No woman chooses to have a life without a husband, without children, without a home,"

Betty said, "unless she's sleeping with her Italian professor."

She realized she'd gone too far the instant the words were out of her mouth. Connie gave her a dirty look: How could you? But she wasn't about to apologize because she had told Giselle again and again that she was making a big mistake, and Giselle refused to take her advice.

"You're so critical," said Connie.

"I am not," Betty answered.

Giselle knew how to get back at her former roommate. "Of course, you are," she said. "You're your mother's daughter. A classic Electra complex. But I don't blame you. I mean, who wouldn't want to murder *your* mother?"

Betty was about to let go another attack when Joan burst into the room.

"How's the Harvard sweetheart?" said Giselle, eager to deflect the focus from herself.

"Divine." Joan kicked off her saddle shoes and sprawled on the floor next to Betty.

"Did you do his homework?" Giselle asked.

Joan smiled. "Of course."

"Would you do mine?" said Giselle.

"No."

"Got an extra ciggie?" Connie asked Giselle.

Giselle pointed to her purse. Connie dug around in the bottom of the bag. Instead of a pack of a cigarettes, she pulled out a plastic saucer-shaped case. Her eyes widened. "This isn't what I think it is, is it?"

Giselle nodded calmly as she opened the case and held up her diaphragm.

"Where'd you get it?" Joan asked.

"The school nurse," Giselle said.

"It's against the law," Betty reminded her.

"Oh, grow up," Giselle said with a dismissive wave of her hand. "It's a girl's best friend."

"A certain kind of girl," Betty said haughtily.

Giselle laughed. "Meet the last virgin bride."

"Spencer is a gentleman."

"Even gentlemen have dicks," said Giselle, hoping to shock Betty with her crude language.

Connie examined the diaphragm in its case. "Maybe I'll get one."

"A dick?" Giselle joked.

"Don't be stupid, Connie," Betty said.

Stung by Betty's implication that she had no use for birth control, that she was "stupid" to think she might need it, Connie stood up and put her cello back in the case. "Someday someone somewhere might be interested," she said, fighting back tears. "Shocking, I know. But just in case, I'll be prepared."

She stamped out of the room and slammed the door behind her.

"Was that necessary?" Joan asked Betty.

Betty hadn't meant anything by her comment. It was a slip of the tongue meant to be well-intentioned advice. She and Connie had been friends since ninth grade at Miss Porter's, and Betty knew that Connie couldn't stay angry long. She felt just a tiny bit sorry that she had upset Connie, but she wasn't about to admit that in front of Giselle and the others. "I was taught that it's best to speak honestly," she defended herself.

"Okay." Giselle shrugged. "You're a bitch."

Betty pretended to ignore her. She picked up her pencil and went back to the seating chart. She thought, Sticks and stones may break my bones . . . but I'm getting married. What do *you* have to show for four years at Wellesley?

Katherine rediscovered an old love at Wellesley—bicycle riding—the favored mode of transportation on campus. At Nancy's suggestion, she bought a secondhand bike for five dollars and began biking to classes, to buy groceries, to explore the countryside by herself or with one of her housemates on weekends when the weather was fine.

She was riding alone one afternoon, pedaling up a hill on a road that skirted Lake Waban.

Cresting the hill, she was breathing hard when she heard a horn beep so loudly behind her that she swerved to the side and barely avoided falling off.

A few hundred yards back, she had seen a sign that announced in big, bold, hard-to-miss lettering: PEDESTRIANS AND BICYCLES ONLY. NO AUTOMOBILES. Now a bright red Alfa Romeo Spyder sped by, the only car on a road where there weren't supposed to be any. Katherine watched the car pass her and wondered what kind of jerk would deliberately disobey the safety rules. A moment later, she realized that she knew the driver, in a manner of speaking. It was Bill Dunbar, the Italian professor she had seen from afar a couple of times since arriving on campus. She stared at the Alfa Romeo as the distance between them widened and saw that he was watching her in his rearview mirror. He gave her a jaunty backhanded wave. Then his car disappeared from sight.

"Wake up, Joanie. Wake up."

Betty's voice was buzzing in her ear like an angry wasp intruding on her dream. Or maybe she was dreaming that Betty was forcing her awake when sleep was all she wanted to do.

"Okay, don't get up," Betty said, which didn't make any sense because then why did Betty keep talking to her when she was asleep? "Don't hear what I have to say about Tommy and Spencer spending the afternoon in New York City at Tiffany's looking at engagement rings."

Joan opened her eyes, and sure enough, Betty was perched on her bed, still wearing her coat and scarf.

Tommy. Tiffany's. Engagement rings. Wide-awake now, she sat up and said, "You're sure?"

Betty nodded. Joan shrieked and threw her arms around her roommate, still not quite believing what Betty was telling her.

"It's everything we ever wanted. We'll be best friends, and our husbands will be best friends, and we'll get houses next to each other, and have babies, and they'll be best friends." Betty bounced on the bed, like a small child unable to contain her excitement. "You're going to be Mrs. Tommy Donegal."

Her dream was about to come true. She loved the sound of the words: "Mrs. Tommy Donegal. When?"

"I'll get the scoop tomorrow," said Betty. She gently pushed Joan back down onto the pillows. "You go back to sleep. I have to finish something." She moved over to her desk and rolled a sheet of paper into her typewriter.

"Now?" Joan asked, snuggling under her quilt. "What are you typing?"

"Shh," said Betty. "Friday's editorial. It's almost done."

Hoop Day. The very words conjured up images of floor-length skirts, petticoats and chignons, sepia-colored photographs. One of the college's quaintest and best-loved traditions, Hoop Day began as part of May Day celebrations, when senior class students, dressed for the first time in their graduation caps and gowns, rolled wooden hoops on the village green. The contest had since been moved to to the beginning of the school year, its location to Tupelo Lane, and the hoops were made of metal, not wood. Otherwise, Nancy explained to Katherine, not much had changed.

Despite the brilliant sun in an azure sky, the air was unseasonably cool on this late October morning. Fallen leaves were swirling on the ground where Katherine stood with Nancy and Violet Albini, the physical education teacher, watching the girl race their hoops.

"It's been going on since the late 1880s," Nancy told Katherine. "Whoever wins is the first to marry."

Katherine was wearing a heavy woolen sweater. She cupped her hands around the mug of cocoa served to her by one of the maids who was circulating among the spectators. "Do the girls take it literally?"

"Only the girl with the winning hoop," said Violet. "Oh, look! It's Phyllis Nayor!"

Loud cheers and applause erupted as Phyllis crossed the finish line. "Good for her! It gets me every time," said Nancy, dabbing at her eyes.

Bill Dunbar was working his way toward them through the crowd. Katherine had run into him on campus about a week after he'd forced her off the road. This time, they were both traveling on foot. He had greeted her like an old friend and made a vague offer to have coffee at some point.

This morning, he didn't bother with pleasantries. He was holding a copy of the school newspaper, *The Daily Wellesley*, and the first words out of his mouth were "Have you seen this?"

"What is it?" asked Katherine, distracted by the sight of Phyllis being lifted onto her friends' shoulders and carried toward Lake Waban.

"A front-page attack on Amanda Armstrong written by Betty Warren. Here." He thrust it into Katherine's hands. "Read it."

Katherine skimmed the lead paragraph. Stunned by the contents, she read aloud, " 'By providing contraception on demand, our school nurse is little more than a cheerleader for promiscuity.' Wow!"

She tried to pass the paper over to Nancy, but Nancy was more interested in Phyllis Nayor's postvictory fate than in Betty's cruel indictment of their housemate.

"Are they really going to dunk her?" Nancy asked. She grimaced sympathetically as Phyllis's cheering classmates tossed her into the chilly water.

"I'm coming, Phyllis!" Violet shouted, running toward the pond.

Nancy tore her gaze from the tableau and turned to Katherine and Bill. "I wouldn't worry. Betty's just a young woman flexing her muscles."

"So was Lizzie Borden," Bill said grimly, "and her mother wasn't president of the Alumni Association."

"Someone please get the poor girl a towel!" Nancy yelled.

"Is Amanda going to get in trouble?" Katherine asked.

"Amanda needs to start minding her p's and q's," said Nancy.

"The trick to surviving Wellesley is never getting noticed," Bill said. He winked at Katherine. "*Ciao,* Mona Lisa."

Nancy frowned. "The big war hero. He thinks he's something special."

"He may be right," Katherine said. "About Wellesley, I mean."

"He sleeps with his students," said Nancy.

Really? And even if he does, is that any of our business? What about poor Amanda? Katherine shivered, but the chill in her bones had no relation to the temperature in the air.

Betty's wedding was two weeks away. Betty's mother was calling her ten times a day. Betty was so nervous she had completely lost her appetite. Her wedding gown was hanging on her like a potato sack because she had lost five pounds since the last visit to the dressmaker.

Wasn't this supposed to be fun? she asked Spencer, who said he thought the fun part came afterward, getting smashed and getting laid. And that if she didn't want to bother with all the wedding crap, they could drive down to Maryland and get married by a justice of the peace.

Betty knew he didn't mean a word of that nonsense. His family had just as many friends and relatives who would die if they couldn't celebrate Betty and Spencer's marriage together. Spencer had a lot on his mind. She shouldn't have bothered him with her silly case of nerves. Everything was going to be absolutely peachy wonderful.

Mrs. Spencer Jones. Oh, how she loved the sound of that!

This morning she had another appointment with the dressmaker. First, she had to drop some things off with her parents, who were meeting with the caterers. She made Joan come with her for moral support, and of course, they were running late for her appointment. She flew into the caterer's office, where Mrs. Warren had the entire staff attending to her every whim and need.

Mrs. Warren grabbed Betty by the arm. She got right down to business: "Did you have the fitting yet?"

Betty skillfully extricated herself from her mother's grasp and said, "We're on our way. Here's the seating chart, and Spencer's list of groomsmen." She was halfway to the door when she delivered her well-rehearsed line. "Oh, I almost forgot. I spoke to Spencer about reading the poem, and he'd rather not. So I said okay."

Betty had spent her life studying her mother so closely that she could read her mind. *Okay? Absolutely not okay.*

Her mother was just about to taste the curried deviled eggs, their caterer's signature hors d'oeuvre. She immediately placed the fork on the table and smiled at Joan. "Excuse us a second, Joan," she said.

Her hand on Betty's arm, as she guided her daughter to a quiet corner, felt like a steel claw.

"A good wife lets her husband think that everything is his idea, even when it's not," she said, summarizing the cornerstone of her beliefs about marriage.

"But I don't care if he reads it," Betty said. In fact, she couldn't remember anymore what mattered to her about the wedding. All she knew was that her mother cared—cared very much—about each and every detail, that Spencer's main concern was that they not run out of champagne, that she just wanted to get one full night's sleep before her wedding day because otherwise she might have a nervous breakdown. And, oh, yes, her father, who would pay any amount for people to satisfy his wife's desires so he didn't have to hear any complaints from her at home. He also wanted to give Betty, his adored only child, the wedding she would remember for the rest of her life.

"You will care in retrospect," Betty's mother told her. "Why don't you see if you can't find a way to nudge the idea into his head? Understood?"

Betty nodded. One more thing to worry about, and the stupid poem—her mother's idea, of course—meant absolutely nothing to her.

Still guiding Betty by the arm, her mother brought her back to the caterer's table. "You must try the salmon mousse," she said.

On cue, the caterer handed each of the girls a cracker covered with a dollop of salmon mousse. It was three fifteen, and they hadn't yet eaten breakfast or lunch, so the mousse tasted delicious.

But Mrs. Warren had more on her agenda than salmon mousse. She was staring intently at their faces, studying them both like specimens under glass.

"Come here, in the light," she ordered. "Both of you. Do you clean your pores?"

"Yes," they said in unison.

"Scrub," she commanded them.

The last straw. Betty couldn't handle any more. She remembered now one of the reasons she was so eager to get married—so she wouldn't have to take any more orders from her mother.

"All right, we have to run." She grabbed Joan's hand and sprinted for the door.

They were giggling so uncontrollably as they drove to the dressmaker that Betty got pulled over by a policeman for running a stop sign. His earnest lecture got them started again after they'd pulled away, hooting and cackling until tears were running down their cheeks and Betty wasn't sure whether she was laughing or crying. Had to be laughing. Because why in the world would she have any reason to cry?

* * *

If Katherine's office were any farther from the center of campus, her mailing address might have been the next town over. Searching for the silver lining, she decided that the extra distance translated into an opportunity for long, healthy walks and bike rides across campus.

The other advantage was that her office was next to an abandoned storeroom, which she quickly annexed and made her own. One wall became a mural-cum–bulletin board, with a constantly changing collage of photos, newspaper articles, drawings, quotations, cartoons, postcards, and greeting cards that amused her on her good days and lifted her spirits when she was feeling down.

Not many students found their way to her office. Most preferred to grab her just before or after class, or when they bumped into her on campus. Joan was among the few willing to make the trek, which included hiking up five flights of stairs.

"I haven't been to this part of campus before," she said, slightly breathless from the climb. "Where are we?"

"No-man's-land," Katherine said. "So to speak."

They shared a laugh at her pun, which broke the ice between them. Katherine had a pretty good idea why Joan had chosen to talk in the privacy of her office, rather than a more public discussion. "Come on in," she said.

As Joan examined her collage, Katherine said, "It's my living room. As in a room . . . with a life of its own."

"What does it mean?"

"Different things on different days. Little bits of my life. People who inspire me. Artists I admire." She pointed to a piece from *The Boston Globe*. "Editorials I don't." She motioned to Joan to take a seat. "You wanted to see me?"

Joan handed her a paper that Katherine had returned the previous day. "You gave me a C."

"I was being kind," said Katherine.

"The assignment was to write about Brueghel. That's what I did."

"No. What you did was copy Strauss."

"I was referencing an expert."

"If I wanted to know what Strauss thought, I'd buy his book," Katherine said. She flipped through one of her books and found a reproduction of Brueghel's *Peasant Wedding*.

"Brueghel was a storyteller," she said. She pointed out some of the details embedded within the painting. "Find the stories. Break them down into smaller pieces. You might enjoy it."

Joan stared disbelievingly at Katherine. "Are you giving me another chance?"

Joan was smart, thoughtful, a leader. Katherine saw something special in her, a quality that set her apart and made the girls want to be around her.

"Is that my file?" Joan pointed to the folder on Katherine's desk. "What does it say?"

Katherine picked it up, read aloud what she knew by heart, "Straight A's . . ."

"Until now."

"President of the poetry society, captain of the debate team, cocaptain of the tennis club, and founder of the Horticulture League."

Joan laughed. "I sound like a pompous ass."

"Yes, but a busy one. *And* you're prelaw? Where are you going to law school?" Katherine said.

She shrugged. "I haven't really thought about that. I mean, after I graduate I plan on getting married."

"And then?"

"Then I'll be married," said Joan.

Katherine glanced at her left ring finger. No engagement ring—at least not yet. "Why choose? Can't you do both? Think about it, for fun. If you could pick any law school in the country, which would you choose? I have a booklet somewhere."

She rooted around for it in the bottom of one of her drawers. She had found a booklet about law schools there and left it, thinking that some of her students might find the information useful.

Joan whispered something inaudible.

Katherine looked up. "I'm sorry?"

"I said Yale. They keep five slots open for women, one unofficially for a Wellesley girl."

Katherine smiled. "But you haven't really thought about it, right?"

She pulled up a chair next to Joan. From what she knew of her, Joan would make one hell of a good lawyer.

Chapter Five

Few situations intimidated Amanda Armstrong, certainly not a meeting with President Carr. Amanda had known Jocelyn Carr for a very long time. They were good, if not close, friends who liked and respected each other. After reading the front page of *The Daily Wellesley*, she wasn't surprised to be called to Dr. Carr's office. But the meeting didn't go at all as Amanda had expected.

Jocelyn was upset for all the wrong reasons. She was excusing Betty's story, instead of naming it for what it was—a finger-pointing diatribe that would have gladdened the heart of the country's top witch-hunter, Senator Joe McCarthy. Amanda wasn't aware of any bad blood between Betty and herself; she couldn't even remember when they had last spoken. But Betty's article was nothing short of a vicious personal attack on her.

"I've been here twenty-one years, Jocelyn," she said. And no one had ever complained about her before.

President Carr nodded. "I can remember you as a student."

"Twenty-four, if you count that," said Amanda. "So why the theatrics? Contraception has been available for years, and you know it."

"Never before on the front page. We cannot appear to promote sexual promiscuity."

This was a side to Jocelyn that Amanda had never known. "It's about appearances, then?" she said, sounding every bit as angry as she felt. "All right, I promise not to appear sympathetic, progressive, or . . . what was it Mrs. Warren said? 'Liberal?' Satisfied?"

President Carr ignored Amanda's sarcasm and spoke in a low, calm voice that belied the emotional content of her words. "I spent the better part of Friday afternoon trying to convince the alumnae that your record was impeccable, that you wouldn't do this again, and that you'd sign a letter saying as much."

Amanda glared at her. "I'm not signing any such—"

"It doesn't matter," Jocelyn interrupted her. She shifted her eyes, then forced herself to meet

Amanda's gaze. "They're letting you go, Amanda," she said.

"They're letting me go? But you're the president," Amanda heard herself pleading and felt diminished.

President Carr stood up. The meeting was over. "Come now, Amanda. Naivete doesn't suit you. I'm afraid the matter is out of my hands."

The news of Amanda's dismissal spread quickly. Nancy told Katherine at dinner. "She's upstairs packing," Nancy said. "She wants to leave as soon as she can."

Katherine didn't have much appetite that evening. She already missed Amanda's presence at the table. Finishing quickly, she helped Nancy with the dishes, then hurried upstairs to Amanda's room.

The door was half open. Katherine didn't bother knocking. She walked in and said, "I heard. I'm sorry."

Amanda's suitcases were open, and her clothes lay in neatly folded piles on the bed. Her eyes were swollen but she managed a smile, and her voice was calm. "Ten years ago, they would have slapped my wrist," she said. "Now there's a committee for the protection of everything."

Katherine shook her head. None of this made any sense. "They think you're dangerous?"

"No, darling, subversive." Amanda laughed mirthlessly. "It's gotten to the point where you don't know who's protecting whom from what." She yanked open another drawer and pulled out her underwear. "I should have left when Josephine died. Really, they're doing me a favor."

The doorbell rang. Katherine heard Nancy greeting guests, and then she heard girls chattering and laughing. Mystified, she looked at Amanda, who gave her a wry smile.

"Ah, the marriage lectures," said Amanda. "She didn't tell you?"

Katherine shook her head.

Amanda grimaced. "I couldn't possibly describe them," she said. "Besides, a picture's worth a thousand words. See for yourself."

Katherine hesitated. Was Amanda sending her downstairs because she preferred to be alone to do her packing? Or did she want the company, but didn't know how to ask Katherine to stay?

"Will you be all right?" she asked Amanda.

"Better than that." Amanda shooed Katherine into the hallway. "Go on now. You're in for a treat." She shook a warning finger at her. "But don't let her talk you into staying."

On an impulse, Katherine gave Amanda a quick kiss on her cheek. Amanda's eyes instantly filled with tears, which she quickly rubbed away with the back of her hand. "Go," she said, giving Katherine no choice. She managed a smile, then hurried back into her room and shut the door.

Katherine wished she had asked Amanda whether she had a place to go, and what she would do next. She hardly knew Amanda, but she had grown very fond of her. She was a kind, caring person with a quirky point of view and a wry sense of humor. A perfect antidote to Nancy's relentlessly upbeat personality.

Katherine felt a nagging concern: Did Amanda have family or friends with whom she could stay? Would she find another job without too much trouble? What must it be like to leave the place that for so long had been her home?

Trying to imagine herself in Amanda's situation, Katherine slowly descended the stairs. Midway down, she looked into the dining room. The table was set for twelve with Nancy's best china and flatware. A formal floral centerpiece sat in the middle of the table, amid a forest of crystal water and wineglasses.

Large cardboard posters leaned against one wall. Each one had a message neatly spelled out in large, bold, capital letters:

HOW TO LEAVE A CAR
HOW TO CROSS AND UNCROSS YOUR LEGS
HOW TO LET A MAN TAKE OFF YOUR OUTER COAT
HOW TO SAY "NO"
HOW TO SAY "YES"

She smothered her laughter and wished she had a camera, so she could send a picture of this scene to Paul.

Nancy turned and noticed Katherine peering over the railing. "Join us?" Nancy pointed to the poster that read: HOW TO SAY "YES."

Katherine had seen enough. She didn't want to offend Nancy. Nancy was a great girl, but Katherine didn't understand this side of her. Nancy sounded as if she actually believed this nonsense. She could talk about "appropriate topics of discussion" and a "husband's future" with a totally straight face, as if her students' future were secondary to and dependent upon their choice of man.

She needed fresh air, a drink, a setting that was more down-to-earth considering Amanda's dismissal. Without bothering to say good-bye to Nancy, she slipped out the door.

The girls eventually quieted down and took their seats around the table. As usual, Joan, Connie, Giselle, and Betty stayed in their own little group. Nancy sat down at the head of the table and smiled graciously, the consummate hostess. She sat up straight, her back well away from the chair, and folded her hands on her lap. She had previously impressed upon the girls that elbows never belonged on the table; when they ate, one hand should always remain in the lap. Now she clapped her hands to command their attention.

Nancy believed that giving the marriage lectures was an honor. She felt privileged to teach the girls how to create an atmosphere of gracious living in their own homes. It wasn't enough for them to be steeped in English literature or American history or art or sociology. They also had to know how to put together the right menu, how to set an inviting table, how to help their husbands advance their careers.

Today she was giving one of her favorite lectures "How to Entertain." She waited until all eyes were on her, then said, "Your husband is at a crossroads in his career. He's competing for a promotion against two rivals, Smith and Jones. To get the edge, you have wisely invited his boss and the boss's wife to a seven o'clock dinner. You have carefully planned your meal, set your table, and arranged for a baby-sitter."

"We have babies?" Giselle broke in.

"I have twins!" Connie sang out.

Nancy ignored them. "Then surprise! It's six fifteen, and your husband calls to say that

Smith, Jones, and their wives have been invited at the boss's request. Always the Wellesley girl, you keep your cool and realize that the boss is probably testing you as much as your husband. What next?"

Although few would admit it, some of the girls believed the marriage lectures were useful. More than a few took notes. But not Giselle, who had no intention of marrying a man unless he could afford a cook, a maid, and a nanny. "What next?" she sang out. "File for divorce!"

She got the hoped-for laughter. Nancy, barely able to keep her visage placid in the face of her fury at the girls for not taking her wisdom seriously, went on. "That's funny. But the thing is, it's not a joke. A few years from now, your sole responsibility will be taking care of your husband and children. You may all be here for an easy A, but the grade that matters most is the one *he* gives you, not me."

"Who's she talking about?" Connie whispered to Giselle.

Giselle rolled her eyes. As if they didn't know . . .

"You'll need to reset your tables, adjust your meal plan, and list appropriate topics of discussion, dividing them into subcategories of premeal, meal, and postmeal banter."

Betty was half listening. She would never admit it, but she was among those who found the lectures not only helpful but also interesting. Today, however, she was too caught up in preparation for her wedding to give her full attention. Her mother had approved her seating plan; today Betty had to fill out the place cards and drop them off at the caterer's office.

At Mrs. Warren's direction, her mother's assistant had typed up a color-coded master list of things to do, and made copies for herself, the caterer, Mrs. Warren, and Betty, so each of them knew who had to do what by when. Betty's mother was having one copy framed, to present it to Betty to hang over her desk, a keepsake of all the hard work that went into planning her wedding.

Betty kept the cards well hidden from Nancy and shielded them with one hand so she could write with the other.

Giselle knew what she was up to. She leaned over and whispered loudly, "Whatever you do, don't put the boss's wife next to your husband."

"Why not?" Betty said, only half listening to Nancy's lecture.

"She's screwing him," Giselle said, shrieking with laughter.

"I hate you," hissed Betty.

Nancy handed out notebooks in which the girls were supposed to create and record their seating plans. She said, "Remember, your husband's future depends on how well you cope. You have thirty minutes, ladies."

"What does she know about husbands?" Connie whispered to Betty.

Betty giggled. "Everything." She gently rubbed her diamond engagement ring, the amulet that kept her safe and protected. "Except how to get one."

Katherine had grabbed her bicycle from the rack. She rode down Main Street, which was almost empty at this hour, and headed for the Blue Ship, a unpretentious bar that often featured a live jazz band.

Bill Dunbar's Alfa Romeo was parked in front of the bar. She went inside and sat down next to Bill at the bar.

He nodded a greeting. "Heard about Amanda," he said. "Sorry, kid."

"She's all right. Better than I'd be," she said. "They sure don't give you a lot of chances here, do they?"

"Depends how much they hate you to begin with," Bill said. "Can I buy you a drink? Or are you here for dinner?"

"How long are the marriage lectures?" she asked, wondering whether he meant to have dinner with her.

Bill waved over the hostess. "Get this woman a booth," he said.

"For two?" the hostess asked.

Bill looked at Katherine. She smiled.

"For two."

They ordered burgers and a bottle of red wine, then found room for apple pie and Irish coffees. Katherine was having a lot more fun than if she'd stayed home with Nancy to learn about seating arrangements and how to let a man take off her outer coat.

After the pie and coffee, Bill had ordered each of them a shot of Scotch. She couldn't think of a good reason not to drink it. The conversation got deeper and more interesting, Bill ordered another round of shots, and she had to hold up her end.

The place had almost emptied out, but Bill didn't seem in a hurry to leave, and she wasn't either. He began talking about his passion for teaching, for introducing his students to a whole other language and culture. "I tried to create a new program where the girls could live in a different country and study the language—"

"Is that where you learned Italian?" she interrupted, interested in hearing more about his past. "In Italy?"

"Yeah," he said, then abruptly changed the subject. "Do you have a boyfriend?"

"Yes." She felt uncomfortable talking about Paul.

"I wouldn't have let you go," he said, swirling what was left of his scotch. "If you were mine."

She glared at him. "I wouldn't have asked permission."

"They say you're progressive," he said, once again switching subjects. "A forward thinker. Are you?"

"They sure do like their labels here. The right families, the right schools, the right art, the right way of thinking."

He grinned and said, "Saves the effort of thinking for yourself."

Sober now and angry, she said, "Why is it all such a joke to you? Don't you care? Don't you want to reach them?"

"Katherine Watson comes to Wellesley and sets us all free? Come on," he goaded her.

Bill was amusing company, but he was being condescending, and her feelings were hurt. She threw down enough money to cover her share of the bill. "Thanks for the drink," she said, standing up to go.

"Take your—" He grabbed her hand. "Wait, Katherine. I was teasing. Look, they have their own way of doing things here. You need to learn to work with them. We all had to."

She turned and glared at him.

"I'm sorry. I didn't mean to offend you. Jeez, you have a temper. Now calm down and finish your drink, Mona Lisa."

"Why do you keep calling me that?" she said,

"Something about your smile."

She threw her head back and laughed a loud, belly-shaking laugh that cleared her head and almost came close to healing her loneliness. Mona Lisa . . . she could be called a lot worse. And flirting with Bill certainly beat listening to another one of Nancy's marriage lectures. He might not have the most squeaky-clean reputation, but he did know how to behave like a gentleman. And then she wondered whose voice she heard in her head. Reputation? Behaving like a gentleman? She hadn't been here six months, and she was already turning into Paul's worst nightmare: a judgmental snob.

"You owe it to the girls to push through your foreign-study program idea," she said.

He laughed, but he sounded angry rather than amused. "I'm two years from tenure. I owe it to myself not to."

"That's a shame," she said, feeling sorry for him.

He laughed again, but this time the laughter didn't sound bitter.

"What?" she said.

"Maybe I will give the overseas study idea another shot. You're right. It is a good idea."

Katherine was surprised, bordering on astonished, to receive an invitation to Betty Warren's wedding. Nancy explained that because Betty's mother was president of the Alumnae Association, the Warrens had invited almost the entire faculty. They were very generous, Nancy had said.

Or maybe ostentatious, thought Katherine.

The ceremony took place at St. John the Evangelist Church in Brookline. A long procession of huge, tail-finned American cars pulled up in front of the church. As Katherine and Nancy walked up the steps, society photographers rushed toward the cars to snap pictures of guests decked out in their most elegant afternoon formal attire. The atmosphere was more in keeping with a coronation than a wedding.

"I'm all in a knot," Nancy said. She had spent hours deciding what to wear. After consulting Katherine and other faculty members and friends, she finally had decided on a ballerina-length blue dress with a matching blue hat.

"You look beautiful," Katherine assured her. "Come on, let's go inside."

A tuxedo-clad usher met them at the door and

asked whether they were friends of the bride or groom. He seated them on Betty's side of the crowded church. A few moments later, Bill slipped into the pew next to Katherine.

"Ever hear the expression keeping up with the Joneses?" he asked.

"Of course." She looked sideways at Bill, who was dressed in a tuxedo, cummerbund, and suspenders.

Bill tilted his head in the direction of the groom's parents. "Mr. and Mrs. Gordon Jones. The actual, historical family they invented the phrase about."

Katherine hid a smile behind her gloved hand. "Good to know. This is quite the event. I can't believe I was invited."

"Look around," Bill said. "Who wasn't?"

As they were ogling the crowd, Giselle came down the aisle with her date. Although she didn't acknowledge either Katherine or Bill, Katherine saw her reach over and very quickly touch Bill's hand.

"One of yours?" asked Katherine.

"No, I had her last year," said Bill.

"I'll bet," she said.

She looked around and caught Joan's eye. Joan pointed to one of the groomsmen and silently mouthed, *That's him.*

Joan had told Katherine about Tommy the

same day she had come by Katherine's office to pick up an application to Yale Law School. When Katherine asked Joan what Tommy thought about her applying to law school, Joan had admitted with some embarrassment that she hadn't yet told him her plan.

Katherine craned her neck to get a good look at Tommy, then smiled at Joan and nodded her approval. Joan next pointed to Spencer Jones, the groom. He was a nice-looking boy, a bit bland faced, but he and Betty made a good couple. A matched set.

The wedding ceremony was predictably high church, distinguished by the radiance of the bride and her elegant bridal party. It was at the dinner reception, held in the grand ballroom of the Boston Copley, that Betty's mother's organizational talents truly bore fruit. Mr. Warren had instructed his wife to spare no expense in planning their daughter's wedding. Mrs. Warren had taken him at his word.

According to Nancy, Betty and Spencer's dinner reception was rumored to be one of the most extravagant ever held in Boston. Nancy, who was remarkably well-informed about such matters, had reveled in reporting to Katherine whatever details Betty had shared with her.

Katherine and Nancy arrived just as the gilded doors to the ballroom were thrown open. The room was magnificently decorated with tier upon tier of flawless white roses, flown in that morning from California. Twenty-five tables for twelve were arranged around the room, allowing plenty of room for the guests to enjoy dancing to the music of a thirty-piece society orchestra.

Betty and her mother had chosen white as the predominant color, not to symbolize innocence, as Bill wryly surmised, but to avoid the cliché-ridden fall color scheme that so many other autumn brides fell prey to. The table linens were off-white, the china was white edged with gold, and the centerpieces were white and pink orchids surrounded by gold candlesticks and white candles.

Nancy and Katherine picked up their place cards. Not surprisingly, they were seated at the same table.

"Come on," said Nancy, leading Katherine through the crowd of chattering guests. "Do you realize who's here? That's J. P. Morgan's grandson. And there's Binky and Boaty of the Philadelphia Biddles. And the governor is right behind you. Don't turn around!"

Katherine had never heard of the Philadelphia Biddles, but Binky and Boaty were attractive girls who seemed on first glance to be relatively normal, despite having been saddled with such strange names. She ignored Nancy's admonition not to stare at the governor, turned, and found him smiling at her, to his wife's apparent disapproval.

Nancy finally located their table. "Here we are, right by the dance floor," she said. She removed her glasses and stuck them in her evening purse. " 'Men seldom make passes at girls who wear glasses,' " she quoted Dorothy Parker, the *New Yorker* writer and charter member of the Algonquin Round Table.

The other guests at their table included Violet Albini and Mrs. Babcock, the housing director.

"Great band." Violet tried to make conversation with a man who happened to be standing next to their table. He nodded and walked away without a word.

She brightened up when Bill appeared. He leaned over to look at the place cards. "Do you mind?" he said to Violet, switching the cards so that he was seated between her and Katherine.

"Not at all." She smoothed down her hair and flashed Bill a bright smile. "Great band."

"I'm getting a Manhattan," Nancy said. "Do you want one?"

Katherine shook her head.

"I'll take a Jack and ginger," Bill said.

Giselle and Connie were standing on the other

side of the room, keeping close tabs on Bill and Katherine.

"He's making his move," Giselle said, her eyes pinned on Katherine. "I knew he'd go for her."

Connie was monitoring Bill's expression. "She's too old for him."

Giselle laughed. "She's too smart for him." She handed Connie her drink. "Hold this," she said. She pulled down the top of her dress to expose more cleavage and patted her hair. She sauntered across the room, doing a passably good imitation of Marilyn Monroe in *How to Marry a Millionaire*.

"Is it your car? Is that how you seduce them?" Katherine teased Bill as Giselle approached.

"I don't seduce anyone," he said, sounding slightly irritated.

Then the band struck up Nat King Cole's hit "Mona Lisa," and he smiled. "They're playing our song," he said.

Before he had a chance to ask Katherine to dance, Giselle was there in front of him, holding out her hand. "Ladies' choice," she cooed.

Katherine smothered a laugh. The girl could not only walk like Monroe, but sound like her, too. But she wasn't going to have a catfight with her over Bill Dunbar. So she waved him away and said, "Ciao," as he danced off in Giselle's arms.

The bride and groom would soon be making their grand entrance. But first, the photographer was shooting them and the rest of the bridal party in various poses. Mrs. Warren had done her homework and hired the most sought-after, most expensive society photographer in New York City. His fee was the equivalent of a down payment on a small house, but Betty and Mrs. Warren thought the expense was justified, given the quality of his work. The framed photographs and wedding album were invaluable keepsakes that they would treasure for decades to come—and eventually hand down to their children.

But the bride and groom were having a tiff. Nothing serious, Mrs. Warren assured the photographer. A case of postceremony nerves and perfectly understandable, given all the pressure they'd been under. She straightened her husband's lapels and whispered to him not to worry—the children would work things out if they had a few minutes.

The photographer wanted his shot. He ordered his assistant to get the couple ready, fight or no fight.

Bride and groom smiled lovingly at each other. "It was your idea," Betty whispered.

"I never said that," Spencer replied sotto voce.

The photographer asked them to hold hands and think happy thoughts.

Betty thought about the cute outfits her mother had bought her at Bergdorf Goodman for her honeymoon in Hobe Sound. "It doesn't matter," she told Spencer. "If you don't want to read the poem, we'll just skip right over it."

Spencer was thirsty. The sooner they were finished taking the damn pictures, the sooner he could get to the champagne. Now there was a happy thought. He shrugged, earning an irritated look from the photographer, and said, "If it's planned, I guess I can say something. I just don't know what."

Another loving smile for the camera.

"I wrote this down, just in case you forgot," Betty said. "It's my favorite."

On any other Saturday afternoon in November, the groom and his ushers would be outside playing football. The groomsmen had willingly sacrificed their game so Spencer could tie the knot, but some of them were feeling cooped up and restless.

People were dancing the rumba and foxtrot in

the main ballroom. Tommy Donegal stuck a loaf of bread under his arm and signaled Charlie Stewart to join him for a game of toss. Their dates, with Giselle tagging along, followed the boys into the other room, where the waiters were cleaning up the remnants of the cocktail party.

The girls gave one another knowing glances: Men! You just have to humor them.

Charlie sent the bread spinning through the air. Tommy jumped, grabbed it, and threw it back.

"Good catch!" shouted Connie, who was Charlie's blind date.

"You said it," said Joan, winking at her friend.

"He's a morsel," Giselle said.

"He's a favor," Connie said sourly. "Remember?"

Joan noticed Katherine leaving the ballroom. "Miss Watson?" she called. "Over here."

Katherine, en route to the ladies' room, stopped to chat. "Hi," she said.

"Hi, Miss Watson," said Connie.

"Having fun?" Giselle asked.

"I wanted you to meet Tommy," Joan said. "Tommy, come here for a second."

Tommy grabbed Joan by the waist and twirled her up in the air. "God, you're beautiful," he said.

Joan was blushing as she extricated herself from his grasp. "Tommy, meet Katherine Watson."

"Wow!" he exclaimed. When he smiled, dimples appeared on both cheeks. "In the flesh. Do you know she hasn't shut up about you?"

"Tommy!" Joan blushed redder, embarrassed by his revelation.

"What?" Tommy ruffled her hair. "She knows what I mean." He turned back to Katherine. "You did something to impress her."

Katherine laughed. "I guess you did, too."

A deep voice, artificially enhanced by a microphone, announced the entrance of the new couple and their parents: "A son is a son till he gets a wife, but a daughter's your daughter . . ."

The crowd shouted out the rest of the lyrics: "For the rest of your life!"

"Mr. Warren," said the master of ceremonies. "How about a dance with your daughter, Mrs. Jones?"

The guests let out a huge cheer of approval.

Joan grabbed Tommy's arm. "C'mon, I want to see," she said.

The band was playing "Oh, My Papa," as Joan, Tommy, and the others ran next door to watch Betty dance with her father. People crowded around the dance floor, applauding the bridal couple and their parents.

"Everybody dance!" the master of ceremonies declared.

Almost immediately, the dance floor filled up with guests who were eager to comply. Nancy weaved through the crowd on unsteady legs, making her way to the bar to order a Manhattan. She had passed tipsy about an hour earlier, but the bartender was cute and the Manhattans were there for the asking. The bartender topped off the drink with a cherry and slid the glass over to her.

"You make these especially well," she said, trying to form a smile.

"Thank you," he said and went back to wiping up the top of the bar.

Nancy took a sip. She felt the whiskey-vermouth combination slipping down her throat to warm the pit of her stomach. "I had a fellow, Lenny," she told the bartender, raising her glass in a halfhearted salute. "You remind me of him so much. He had this funny thing with his two front teeth overlapping, just like you."

The bartender forced himself to smile. He was tired and ready to go home. Mixing drinks was his part-time job. The rest of the time he was a scholarship student at Harvard Medical School. He was practically a teetotaler himself, but a buddy of his knew the caterer. He'd been hired because women liked his face and tended to order more drinks when he was working the bar.

"He's dead now," Nancy said. "South Pacific."

Her glass, which had been full just a minute ago, was empty. She held it up to the bartender. Time for another one.

The band had stopped playing. The guests had been served fresh glasses of champagne. The microphone had been turned over to the groom. Betty stood next to Spencer, her sweet, radiant face a study in dewy-eyed bewilderment: What on Earth was Spencer up to?

Spencer held up his hand, asking for quiet. He raised his glass to Betty and said, "I thought of a million ways to try to tell you, Betty, how I feel. But instead I defer to your favorite poem:

> "O, my luve's like a red, red rose,
> That's newly sprung in June.
> O, my luve's like the melodie
> That's sweetly play'd in tune.
>
> As fair art thou, my bonie lass
> So deep in luve am I
> And I will luve thee still, my Dear
> Till a' the seas gang dry.

Till a' the seas gang dry, my Dear
And the rocks melt wi' the sun!
O I will luve thee still, my Dear
While the sands o' life shall run."

Spencer managed to get through the entire Robert Burns poem, although he mispronounced some words and lost much of his audience after the first stanza. Betty was smiling so hard her face hurt. When she saw that her mother was crying, she began to cry, although she didn't know why. She didn't much like the poem, but her mother claimed it was a Warren tradition because her father, who was one-quarter Scots and had threatened to wear a kilt today, had recited it at his wedding to Betty's mother.

The Warrens knew how to throw a great party. Everything was first-class: the location, the food, the band, the guest list. The dance floor was packed with dozens of handsome couples: beautiful, accomplished girls, fine-looking young men with solid-gold prospects, their parents and grandparents, for whom money and power was their due.

"My parents say that my future is right on the horizon," Charlie Stewart told Connie. He whirled her around the floor and bent her backward so that her head almost touched the floor.

"Tell them the horizon is an imaginary line that recedes as you approach it," said Connie, giggling breathlessly as she twirled herself into his arms.

Charlie laughed, and they both applauded when the music ended.

"Thank you," said Connie. "I had a really nice time."

"Is this the brush-off?"

"No, of course not." As if she would ever dump a boy like Charlie. "I thought you were, you know, done . . . with me."

The band started up again, playing "You Belong to Me."

Charlie looked bewildered, like a little boy who had lost his teddy bear. "Why would you think that?"

"Betty said"—Connie forced herself to finish the sentence—"I just don't want to take advantage. I know this is just some favor."

"She did me the favor, not you." Charlie put his arms around her and kissed her lips, first lightly, then as if he meant what he was saying. And then they were dancing, and he couldn't hold her any tighter than he already was.

They were dancing so closely together that

Connie didn't notice when Katherine walked past, all by herself. But Bill saw her, and he couldn't tear his eyes away from her.

"She's too good for you," said Giselle, coming up behind him.

"You're probably right," Bill said.

Giselle held out her arms, an invitation to dance. "I'm too good for you, too, but I have lower expectations."

"I thought we settled this last spring, Giselle," he said. But his arms were around her and they were dancing.

She pushed herself closer against him and nestled into his arms. "Then you shouldn't have slept with me over the summer."

Katherine was spared the sight of Bill and Giselle renewing their friendship. She was intent on finding Nancy, whom she finally tracked down at the bar. The band was playing "How Much Is That Doggie in the Window." But Nancy didn't join in the chorus, nor was Katherine laughing when she found her friend slumped over the bar, a half-empty highball glass in front of her.

"Are you ready?" Katherine grabbed Nancy's shoulders and tried to help her from the barstool.

Nancy shrugged her off. Slurring her words,

she said, "Do you wanna hear something funny? Lenny's not dead. Technically speaking."

Nancy's car was in the valet-parking section. Katherine somehow had to get her outside and into the car. "Okay, let's go." She pushed the stool one hundred eighty degrees so that Nancy was facing her.

"He got married," Nancy said, flopping backward against the bar. "He got kids and a mortgage. It was all supposed to be mine"—she hiccuped and gave Katherine a lopsided grin—"except the wife."

"I know. Come on," Katherine said quietly, consolingly, the way she might talk to a young child. She took a small evening bag from the bar. "Is this yours?"

Without waiting for an answer, she grabbed the bag and took Nancy under the arms so she could make her stand up.

"Leave me alone!" Nancy shouted.

A knot of guests standing nearby looked to see who was causing the commotion. Nancy was oblivious to their stares.

"You don't look like him at all, you ugly bartender! You couldn't shine his shoes!" she yelled at the young fellow who'd been serving her all night.

"Nancy, stop it," Katherine said firmly.

Nancy tried to stand up, stumbled, and fell to her knees. "It wasn't supposed to turn out like this," she sobbed. She glared at the bartender. "You were supposed to choose me."

Katherine put her arm around Nancy's shoulders and stroked her cheek. Nancy was crying loudly. Katherine, too, could barely hold back her tears.

"I know, honey," she said, rocking Nancy back and forth. "I know."

Chapter Six

A friend of a friend owned a small gallery in the warehouse district near Boston Harbor. Katherine spent a few blissful hours there talking shop with the owner, Joe O'Neil, a Jackson Pollock fan who had actually visited Pollock at his home on eastern Long Island. "The guy's a genius," O'Neil said. "He can't hold his liquor, but he's a damn genius." Then he offered Katherine another glass of the cheap red wine he'd been drinking all afternoon and told her to bring her girls over anytime. "Let's show those Wellesley chicks the future of art in the twentieth century."

Katherine didn't wait long to take him up on his offer. She wanted her students to experience Abstract Expressionism in a gritty, unembellished setting, rather than the hushed, reverential museum atmosphere.

A cold November rain was falling the morning of their field trip. The gray sky and chill wind off the water heightened the sense that they were headed into unknown territory. Even the girls who had grown up around Boston hadn't ever ventured into this part of town.

The street was paved with the original nineteenth-century cobblestones; the city hadn't yet developed the area. Huge trucks lined both sides of the curb. The Teamsters hauling heavy cartons and racks of merchandise stared openly at Katherine and her entourage of well-dressed young women who were carefully picking their way through the muddy streets. The women seemed as out of place in this rough, working-class district as a flock of seagulls in the middle of an Iowa cornfield.

The whole class—except for Betty, who was still on her honeymoon—crammed themselves into the freight elevator, sharing the space with a woman whose cart was loaded down with coffee, tea, oversize cheese-and-salami sandwiches, and gooey pastries.

"I had a dream like this once," Connie said, as the elevator creakily rose to the fifth-floor gallery. "It didn't end well."

The gallery was formerly a leather factory

whose owner had gone bankrupt. His name was still on the door: DIRNFELD LEATHER GOODS. Wooden crates contained recently delivered canvases. Large pieces of factory equipment, cutters and stampers, stood in another corner of the room, next to piles of leather belts and key chains, which Joe had acquired from the Dirnfelds along with the space.

Katherine hugged Joe. "Thanks so much for this. You're a pal."

The girls gaped at Joe, who was dressed in a black T-shirt, tight black jeans, and black high-top sneakers.

"Behold, my darling," he said. "There it is."

He pointed across the room to an enormous, paint-strewn picture waiting to be hung. The canvas was spattered with gobs of black and white paint that appeared to be randomly strewn, with no sense of coherence or form.

Giselle gaped at it. "That's Jackson Pollock?" she said.

"In a word," said Susan.

"But what's the point?" Joan asked. "I mean, it's thick drops of paint."

Connie looked incredulous. "I was just getting used to the idea that dead, maggoty meat was art. Now this?"

"Please tell me we don't have to write a paper about it?" Susan begged.

Katherine tried to hide her exasperation. She said, "Do me a favor. Do yourselves one. Stop talking and just look. You don't have to like it or write about it, but you are required to consider it. That's the only assignment for today. When you're done, you may leave."

Without another word, Susan headed straight for the elevator. She leaned on the button and shifted impatiently from one foot to the other as she waited for the elevator to arrive. A few other girls followed her lead. But the rest, their curiosity piqued, clustered around Katherine.

"What do you think, Miss Watson?" Joan asked.

"I think I need to stand here awhile," said Katherine. She could have stood there all day, studying Pollock's juxtaposition of light and dark, surface and depth. She felt in the presence of a vision too new and raw to be categorized or defined. Genius, pure and simple. As a teacher, she was supposed to convey the significance of the work. But she lacked the words to make her students understand that Pollock was almost single-handedly transforming the face of modern art. The girls had to glimpse this truth for themselves, or not see it at all, until they were ready to open their eyes.

"May I stand with you?" Joan asked, speaking as quietly as if she were standing in a church.

"Me, too," said Giselle.

Katherine turned to Connie, who stood squinting at the painting from across the room. "What about you, Connie? What do you have to say?"

Connie grinned. "I say, thank God Betty's not here."

Connie had studied the cello since she was nine years old. Her parents had thought she would outgrow her interest in it, but the opposite had occurred. She was more devoted than ever to playing her instrument. No one ever had to remind her to practice; the hours she spent alone practicing were among her happiest. All she needed was an empty room, a chair, her bow, and the cello between her legs. When she drew the bow across the strings, she entered her own private space, where no one could intrude or distract her.

Which was why, when she finished playing "What'll I Do?," a favorite Irving Berlin song, she was jarred, as if startled awake from a deep sleep, by the sound of applause at the back of the otherwise empty rehearsal room. The source of the applause was equally jarring.

"Where did you come from?" she asked Charlie Stewart,

"Mars," he said, grinning as he walked toward her.

"What a coincidence," she said, trying to recover her composure.

"Donegal came by to see Joan," he explained. "I hopped a ride."

She couldn't help herself. She had to ask, "Why?"

He walked right up to her chair and leaned over. "So I could do this," he said.

She forgot to breathe as his lips found hers. His skin smelled fresh and ocean scented, like the November wind and fog. Their kiss lasted forever, but not long enough. When they drew apart, she stared into his blue eyes and saw feelings there that mirrored her own.

But she was scared, too. She didn't want to care so much. Charlie had taken her to the wedding as a favor to Betty and Spencer, and she didn't want to lose her heart to a friend of Spencer Jones.

Charlie patted her on the head, stuck his hands in his pockets, and walked away without even saying good-bye. Connie instantly burst into tears—tears of happiness and fear and wonderment. And most of all, disbelief. What could a guy like Charlie possibly see in her?

Christmas vacation sneaked up on Katherine. First came exams, which had to be marked before semester break. Then she had to buy presents for Paul and some friends back home, as well as for Nancy, Bill, and a few other Wellesley friends. Before she realized it, the girls were packing up to go home, and she had made no plans for herself.

Nancy had begged Katherine to spend Christmas in Duxbury with her family, but Katherine politely declined the invitation. She had gone to Duxbury for Thanksgiving and didn't want to impose again. Or so she told Nancy. The truth was that Nancy's family, though pleasant, was so formal and reserved that she didn't feel comfortable around them. The prospect of a solitary Christmas without the tree and other trimmings felt less lonely than Christmas at the Abbeys', who didn't seem to care about or have much in common with one another.

Katherine was taking a short cut through the administration building a few days before Christmas break when President Carr tapped her on the shoulder. "Katherine," she said. "Do you have a minute? Walk with me."

Katherine smiled. She would have had to be in an awful tearing hurry before she would refuse the president's company.

"Are you going home for the holidays?" asked President Carr.

She shook her head no.

"Too far?"

"Too expensive. Besides, I've never had a New England Christmas," she said, pausing at the front door of the building to put on her leather gloves.

President Carr laughed. "Our weather hasn't scared you away then?"

"I love it here," Katherine said, without hesitation.

"Why?"

Katherine glanced sideways at President Carr. An odd question, one she felt obligated to answer. "Do I love it? Because I do. I love the girls. I love teaching them."

They stepped out into the icy cold air. The sky was gray, the wind sharp. Katherine shivered and wound her scarf more tightly around her neck.

"I've gotten calls about some of your methods," President Carr said, "They're a little unorthodox for Wellesley. We're traditionalists, Katherine."

"Yes, I know," she said, trying to hide her shock. She felt ambushed. She hadn't gotten any feedback from Dr. Staunton, so she had naively assumed that her curriculum changes were acceptable.

President Carr nodded at a group of students passing by, then turned back to Katherine. "If you'd like to stay on . . ."

Katherine Watson arrives at Wellesley.

Class is in session.

The girls gather around the dorm room to gab.

Katherine instructs the students on the finer points of art history—and life.

Katherine looks on as Betty and Spencer Jones get married.

Joan Brandwyn and Betty Jones, née Warren, discuss the future.

Katherine confronts Betty.

Katherine finds a soul mate in fellow faculty member Bill Dunbar.

Katherine takes her students out for a field trip.

Katherine challenges her students to look deeper and reflect upon art.

Katherine enjoys the balmy spring weather on the bank of Lake Waban.

The girls decide to surprise Katherine.

Katherine is surrounded by her appreciative students.

Joan Brandwyn thanks Katherine for supporting her in her application for law school.

Mike Newell lends direction to an upcoming scene.

"Was there a question?" She heard the shakiness in her voice.

"More a discussion," President Carr said.

"About me? About keeping me here?" Anger replaced hurt. She imagined President Carr, Dr. Staunton, Betty Wilson's mother, maybe other members of the art department, sipping tea around the conference table, critiquing her innovations and sniping about her avant-garde approach to art history.

"You'll be given a formal review in May. Until then, a little less modern art, yes?" President Carr smiled at her, not unkindly, and held her gaze, as if waiting for Katherine's response. After what felt like a very long time, but probably was no more than a few seconds of silence, the president smiled again, less warmly, and said, "Happy holidays."

Katherine watched her walk down the path, greeting students and faculty members. "Happy," she said aloud. She had thought she could be happy at Wellesley. But happy suddenly felt like a very distant planet in the solar system.

Nancy had insisted on throwing an early Christmas party, complete with a tree, figgy pudding, and mulled apple cider. Each invitee had to draw the name of another guest, then play that person's secret Santa and buy him or her a small, funny present.

Katherine's secret Santa had chosen a small reproduction print of van Gogh's *Sunflowers.* The night before Christmas Eve, with few people left on campus, she sat down at her desk with the van Gogh kit and lost herself in the vibrant swirls and powerful emotion inherent in the art. It gave her an idea—she set up a small canvass and some paint, and set to work trying to reproduce the artwork for herself.

Someone knocked on her door. Nancy poked her head inside. "Guess who has an early Christmas gift?" Her smile faded as she noticed the mess. "How do you live like this?"

Katherine glanced around. "Like what?" she said, unperturbed.

The door opened wider. For an instant, Katherine thought she was hallucinating.

"Hey, you!" said Paul

"Hey!" Katherine jumped up and ran screaming into his arms.

"We'll just have to wait for you to tidy up," Nancy said, pretending to pull Paul out of the room.

"In our lifetime?" Paul laughed. "That'll never happen. Come here, beautiful."

He wrapped himself around her and gave her a kiss that told of long days and nights wishing she were there with him.

Nancy couldn't tear her eyes from them. It was as if she'd never before seen two people kiss. Then, suddenly embarrassed, she tiptoed out of the room and, quietly closing the door, left them to get reacquainted in private.

Some time much later, Katherine realized it was getting late, and Paul remembered that he hadn't eaten any dinner. They went out into the night and headed for the Blue Ship for hamburgers and beer. He had so many questions for her. She had so much to tell him, things he could understand better than any of her friends at Wellesley.

"You know how back home they had a few hundred students in each class?" she said. "Jammed in, standing room only?"

Paul nodded. She'd complained constantly about the overcrowding.

"Well, here it's maybe twenty girls."

"Privilege." He shrugged. "You still like it though?"

"You get to know them. Whether you want to or not." She glanced at him by the light of the streetlamp. "Hey, your lips are turning blue." Paul was unprepared for winter in Massachusetts. She opened her coat and wrapped it around him. "Come in and get warm."

Intertwined beneath her coat, they hurried into the Blue Ship. Neither of them noticed Giselle huddled in the shadows, smoking a cigarette and shivering from the cold.

She saw them, and she also saw Bill, whom she'd been waiting for, drive up to the tavern.

"Bill?" Giselle greeted him as he got out of his car.

He did a double take. He hadn't seen her hiding there in the dark. "What are you doing out here?"

"Freezing." She laughed mirthlessly.

Bill shook his head. "Jesus, is this ever going to end?" he said. "It's over, Giselle. You have to stop following me."

She looked at him with pleading eyes. "I just need to talk a little. Please?"

"All right," he conceded. "One drink. Then you go home alone. Agreed?"

Giselle nodded gratefully and followed him inside. All she needed was one more chance.

Paul wanted privacy, so he and Katherine took a corner booth. He leaned across the table and held her hand.

"You're beautiful," he said, folding her fingers around his.

"You're insane," she said happily.

"I missed you."

"Me, too," she said, realizing it was true.

"Life without you isn't life," Paul said.

Katherine looked away. When she raised her eyes, she saw Bill Dunbar and Giselle coming into the bar.

"I don't want to go through life not living," Paul said, "do you?" When her eyes filled up with tears, Paul reached into his pocket and brought out a tiny tissue-wrapped package. "I love you so much. Enough to move to this elitist icebox if you want me to."

Inside the box was a small, gleaming diamond ring. "Make an honest man out of me," he said.

She was so shocked that she couldn't find the words to respond. "Paul . . ." She struggled to formulate a thought. "Oh, my God! This is such a—"

"Hi, Miss Watson," Giselle said, suddenly standing in front of her and ruining the moment.

Katherine gaped at Giselle, unable for a fraction of a second to recall her student's name. However she had meant to finish the sentence, the thought had disappeared.

She returned to reality with a heavy thud. Bill Dunbar was standing next to Giselle.

"Oh, hi. Bill Dunbar, Giselle Levy, this is my—"

"Fiancé, as of two minutes ago." Paul stood up and shook Bill's hand. "Paul Moore, nice to meet you."

Bill stared at Katherine. He looked as stunned as she had felt just minutes earlier.

Giselle, on the other hand, was ecstatic. "Two minutes? How romantic!" she gushed. "Congratulations! Have you set a date?"

Paul grinned. "I don't think she's caught her breath."

"No, I haven't . . . we haven't . . . no, no date." Katherine's brain didn't seem to be properly functioning.

"Sit down," Paul said. "We'll have a toast."

Giselle was about to slide into the booth, but Bill clamped his hand on her shoulder. "Love to, but we're in a hurry and . . . you know . . . But that's great. Just great. For both of you." He shook Paul's hand. "Congratulations, old man. C'mon, Giselle, we have to go."

Giselle looked as if she'd just been given the best Christmas present ever. "Merry Christmas," she said with a blissful smile. "And the best of tidings to you both."

Katherine needed so desperately to be alone in her room that she would have run barefoot through the icy streets if that could have gotten her home faster. Pleading exhaustion from all the excitement, she told Paul she had to leave. Paul said he understood. He, too, was looking forward to getting back to her place.

The cold forced them to walk quickly without too much talk, but holding hands was pleasure enough for the moment. As soon as they came into the house and shrugged off their jackets, Paul headed up the stairs.

"No, Paul." Katherine touched his arm to stop him from getting any farther. "We have house rules. Men aren't allowed upstairs."

"Come on." He was sure she was joking.

"No," she said, almost as confused as he was about her decision.

"Why?" He sounded puzzled, not yet angry, but halfway there.

"Because I'm not comfortable." Her explanation was a half-truth that explained nothing. She walked into the television room and began taking the cushions off the sofa. "This is a convertible bed. I'll make it up for you."

"What are you . . . ?" He laughed, figuring this was some kind of dumb joke she was playing on him. But as she hurriedly removed the rest of the cushions, he realized she was completely serious. "You're not kidding. I came three thousand miles to see you, and I'm sleeping down here? Alone?"

She pulled sheets and blankets out of the closet, threw them onto the sofa bed, and quickly tucked the corners of the sheets under the mattress. She shoved pillows into the cases.

She was behaving like a woman with the threat of a gun held to her head if she didn't accomplish a dangerous task.

"Can you stop?" Paul grabbed a pillow from her and threw it onto the bed. "Just stop what you're doing for one second and tell me what the hell's going on," he said, his voice rising with anger.

She picked up the pillow and pressed it against her chest. "I don't know," she said, shaking her head, as if trying to dislodge her sense of panic. "I feel like my life's gotten away from me. We haven't seen each other for three months, and suddenly there's a ring on my finger."

"And that makes you uncomfortable, too?"

She sat down and rubbed the back of her neck, wishing they weren't having this conversation. She hated what she was about to say, but she had always been honest with Paul, and she wasn't going to change the rules of their relationship. "Last time I checked, our train wasn't on that track," she said.

Paul looked so sad that it took all her self-control not to reach for his hand and comfort him. "When was the last time you checked?" he said.

After pausing for a moment, he continued, "You always think there's somewhere better to be, some big thing you haven't done, some crusade to lead. But I'm starting to think all that stuff is just a way to avoid real life."

He turned to leave, and she got even more frightened that he knew her better than she knew herself and that the best thing in her life was about to vanish.

"Wait, Bill," she cried. "Don't leave."

"The name's Paul." He scowled at her, and his voice shook with anger.

She would rather have had a fight than see how badly she'd wounded him with the slip of her tongue. "Paul . . . I'm not saying no to you."

He shrugged his shoulders, pretending insouciance. "You're not saying anything. You never really do."

In honor of her first Christmas as Mrs. Spencer Jones, Betty had gone all out decorating their house in Cambridge. She'd driven to a tree farm in Sudbury and chosen the tallest, greenest tree she could find. The sad part was that Spencer couldn't come with her. She'd imagined them picking out the tree together, one of their first traditions as a married couple. But Spencer had to work late at the law firm almost every night, so she'd gone alone and had the tree delivered as a surprise.

She hung two stockings on the fireplace mantel and filled them both with lots of little funny toys and gag items. She got up on a stool and hung a sprig of mistletoe over the entrance to the living room. She baked trays of special Christmas cookies from recipes her mother gave her, and she put bowls of chocolate Santas and reindeers and candy canes in the living room, TV room, and even in their bedroom.

She begged Spencer to help her choose Christmas tree ornaments, but once again he was too busy with work. So she bought some of them by herself, the rest when she went shopping with Joan and her mother. Spencer loved the tree. He said so when he came home from the office and found the tree with all the decorations in place.

"Didn't you want me to help you?" he asked Betty. She kissed him and smiled. No point reminding him she'd asked him to help, but he'd been too busy.

Spencer was so pleased with how the house looked that he suggested she invite Joan and Tommy for dinner. Betty consulted her mother about the menu and decided on leg of lamb with mint jelly and roasted potatoes. For her first official dinner party, she took out the white linen cloth, the good china, and her grandmother's silver. Spencer wanted beer not wine, so she compromised by making eggnog and fruitcake with hard sauce.

Basking in her friends' compliments as they finished the fruitcake and cookies, Betty felt rewarded for all her hard work by the look of pride on Spencer's face.

She brought in a tray of coffee and more cookies just in time to hear Tommy say, "What's the big hush-hush secret? Are we going to hear the pitter-patter of a little Spencer?"

"Tommy, stop," Joan scolded. "They'll tell us when they're ready." She looked sideways at Spencer. "Are you ready?"

"Is she the cutest?" Tommy demanded of his friends. "You're the cutest. Look at that face. I love that face. Come here, you." He pulled Joan to him and kissed her.

Embarrassed by their public display of affection, Betty and Spencer watched in awkward silence.

"No little Spencer, not yet," Betty finally said. "But big Spencer was just made a junior partner."

"It's about time," Tommy said, reaching across the table to shake his friend's hand.

"And it's a significant raise, too!" Betty proudly announced.

Spencer gave his wife a disapproving glance. "Betty!" he chided her.

Betty felt the color rising to her cheeks. She hated when Spencer criticized her. "I can say that to Joan and Tommy, can't I? Anyway, it is a good raise, so maybe a family isn't far behind." She began clearing the table. "Why don't you boys go smoke your cigars in the den and we'll just wash up?"

"I'll help," said Joan, gathering up the glasses.

Spencer and Tommy moved across the hall to the den and left the girls to take care of cleaning up the kitchen. Joan followed Betty into the kitchen.

"Look at this," said Betty, walking into the service porch. She pointed to her brand-new washer and dryer. "Ta-da!" she sang out.

Joan gently stroked the top of the washing machine. "Beautiful," she said. "You are so lucky. You have everything we ever dreamed of."

"You will, too," Betty assured her.

Joan was quiet for a moment. Then she said, "I have a secret. Swear you won't gab? To anyone?"

Betty's eyes widened. She crossed her heart, the gesture they'd used since childhood to pledge absolute secrecy.

Joan closed the kitchen door and lowered her voice. "I've been accepted early to Yale Law School," she said.

"To what?" Betty shrieked. "Why? You don't want to be a lawyer!"

Joan put her hand over Betty's mouth. "Shh. Maybe I do," she said.

Betty was aghast. "You won't switch brands of cold cream without asking me, but you applied to law school?"

"On a lark," Joan said sheepishly. "We never thought I'd get in."

"Who's 'we?' "

"Miss Watson. She practically filled out my application." Joan explained how Katherine not only arranged to get Joan the necessary forms, but had also provided invalvable advice on how to position herself in the application.

"You have to be kidding!" Betty was so agitated that she picked up a gingerbread man from the plate of cookies and bit off his head. "What right does she have? You're getting married!"

Joan wiggled her left hand in front of Betty. "First of all, there's no ring on my finger. Secondly, I can do both."

Two more bites and the gingerbread man lost his legs. "How does Tommy feel about that?" Betty said.

"He doesn't know. No one does."

Betty swallowed the rest of the cookie. "Not even her?"

"No one!" Joan assured her oldest friend.

"Joan?" Tommy yelled from the den. "Betty? How about more coffee?"

Betty grabbed the percolator from the stove; she put it on the tray she'd prepared earlier with cups and saucers, and added another plate of cookies. "You are this close to having everything you ever wanted," she said sternly, pushing the door open with her foot. "And this close to losing it."

Joan put her finger to her lips, reminding her of her pledge. Betty rolled her eyes, but nodded. She had pledged silence, and she wouldn't go back on her word. She came into the den wearing her warmest hostess smile. But the smile quickly disappeared when she saw Spencer's overnight bag on the floor.

"I just got a call," he told her. "They need me in New York tomorrow," he said.

First, Joan's ridiculous announcement, and now Spencer was ruining their first dinner party by deserting her. It was all too much for Betty. "But Tommy and Joan are here. Can't you please leave in the morning?" she said, blinking back tears.

Spencer shook his head as he shrugged on his coat and grabbed his hat. "I'd miss the meeting. Sorry, you guys. Can we take a rain check?"

"Sure, buddy," Tommy said.

"We'll see you after the New Year. Merry and happy." Spencer blew a kiss to Joan and slapped Tommy on the back. He gave Betty a quick kiss on the cheek. "I'll call you in the morning," he promised. And then he was gone.

A cold snap arrived from Canada the week between Christmas and New Year's. A blanket of clouds settled in, and the sky turned slate gray. No matter how many layers of clothes she put on, Katherine couldn't get warm. She turned up the heat in her room, huddled under the blankets, but her bones ached from the chill, and her soul longed for the sun. She tortured herself with memories of Christmas in Los Angeles: blue skies, fragrant eucalyptus trees, seventy-degree weather.

Determined not to spend the week in bed, she pulled on her woolen underwear and snow boots and took brisk walks around the campus. There wasn't a soul around, except for an occasional campus cop or handyman. When her teeth began to chatter from the cold, she went to the library and tried to lose herself in the stacks. She was feeling almost warm until she caught a glimpse of Bill wandering through the stacks a few feet away. She ducked down so he couldn't see her. As soon as he disappeared from view, she wondered why she was trying to avoid him and wished he would call and invite her out for a drink.

With Nancy gone and the food service people on vacation, Katherine had to fend for herself if she wanted to eat. She found a diner with decent burgers and ate breakfast and dinner there. But the torn, tatty Christmas decorations and the badly recorded carols were more depressing than eating chocolate bars, popcorn, and Ritz crackers with peanut butter in her bedroom.

Just before New Year's Eve, a snowstorm brought a foot of snow, heavy winds, and falling temperatures. After hours spent reading, sleeping, and watching jumbo-size snowflakes swirl past her window, Katherine ran out of peanut butter. She felt creaky from lack of exercise, so she dressed as if for an Arctic expedition and trudged out into the storm to restock her provisions.

The snow was deeper than she'd expected. The wind whipped her muffler around her face. Momentarily disoriented, she lost her balance and landed in a drift. Buried up to her knees, she looked up at the leaden gray sky and cried out, "Where have you gone?"

A campus security guard, assigned the hopeless task of shoveling the walks, trudged over to rescue her. He studied her face: who was this screaming lunatic?

"Sorry," she said, as he helped her up. "I was talking to the sun."

Would the sun ever shine again in Massachusetts?

Chapter Seven

The snow was still falling when the students returned to campus in January. Desperate for sun in any form, and inspired by her secret Santa gift, Katherine chose to open second semester with a discussion of van Gogh. And just for a change of pace, she decided to teach the class in her office.

Holding up an oversize art book, she opened to a reproduction of one of van Gogh's most famous paintings and asked Joan to read the caption.

"*Sunflowers,* Vincent van Gogh, 1888."

"He painted what he felt, not what he saw," said Katherine. She turned the page to the next plate, *Starry Night,* and gave the girls time to study it.

Then she said, "But people couldn't understand. To them it was crude and childlike. It took years for them to see his technique. Look closer. The brush strokes seem to make the night sky move."

She flipped to the next page: *Self-Portrait*.

"Yet he never sold a painting in his lifetime. Look at his self-portrait. There's no camouflage, no romance. Honesty. And now sixty years later, where is he?"

"Famous?" Giselle called out.

"So famous that everyone has a reproduction," said Katherine. "There are postcards—"

"We have the calendar," Connie said.

Katherine nodded. "There you go. With the ability to reproduce art, it's now available to the masses. People no longer need to own van Gogh originals."

"We do," Susan whispered. "In the Newport house."

Her classmates stared at her.

"But it's small," she assured them. "Tiny."

Katherine held up the paint-by-numbers box of *Sunflowers* she'd received for Christmas. "They can paint their own. Van Gogh in a box, ladies, the newest form of mass-distributed art. Paint by numbers."

She handed the box to Connie and motioned her to read the copy on the box.

Connie imitated the voice of a radio huckster. " 'Now everyone can be van Gogh! It's so easy! Just follow the simple instructions and in minutes you're on your way to being an artist!' "

Katherine took three completed paint-by-numbers pictures from the box. She leaned them against the blackboard in the front of the room.

"Ironic, isn't it?" she said. "Look what we've done to the man who refused to conform his ideals to popular taste, who refused to compromise his integrity. We've put him in a little box and asked you to copy him. The choice is yours, ladies. You can conform to what others expect of you, or you can—"

"I know." A voice came from the back of the room. Betty stood posed in the doorway. "Be ourselves?"

The girls squealed with excitement. Betty hadn't been to classes since just before her wedding. Connie jumped up and hugged her. "You're a sight for sore eyes," she said.

"I would have been here sooner, but silly me, I thought class was held in the classroom," she said, looking pointedly at Katherine. "Love the hair, Suze."

Susan beamed. A compliment from Betty was a rare and valuable prize.

"Glad you could join us, Mrs. Jones," said Katherine. "I thought we'd lost you."

Betty rolled her eyes, but otherwise didn't deign to reply.

"There's sort of this unwritten rule here for the married girls," Connie began.

"Don't bother." Betty dismissed the need for an explanation.

Katherine was furious, but she kept her voice calm as she consulted her records. "Since your wedding, you've missed six classes, a paper, and your midterm," she said.

"Well, thank God I caught the paint-by-numbers lecture!" Betty said, mugging for her friends. "I was on my honeymoon, and then I had to set up house." She swung herself up onto a desk and asked the class, "What does she expect?"

"Attendance," Katherine said.

"Most of the faculty turn their heads when married students miss a class or two," Connie said, trying to be helpful.

Katherine was appalled. How could the administration sanction such a ridiculous idea? And why would the students want such a dispensation? Their parents were paying a fortune for them to attend classes. Didn't they want to get the most for their money?

"Why not get married in your freshman year?

That way, you could graduate without ever stepping foot on campus." She wondered whether any of them grasped the idiotic logic behind the custom.

"Don't disregard our traditions just because you're subversive," Betty sniped.

"Don't disrespect this class just because you're married," Katherine said, gritting her teeth to keep from saying anything more.

"Don't disregard me just because you're not."

The girls looked shocked. Betty was known for testing the limits, but this time she really had gone too far. Their eyes darted back and forth between teacher and student, hanging on every volley as if they were watching a tennis match at Forest Hills. Next serve: Katherine Watson.

Katherine's palms itched to haul off and smack Betty across the face. She knew better, of course. She had nothing to gain, everything to lose, by engaging in a spitting match with her student. "Come to class. Do the work. Or I'll fail you," she said, sounding much calmer than she felt.

Betty pulled off her hat and fluffed up her hair. "If you fail me, there will be consequences," she said.

"Are you threatening me?" Katherine almost laughed at the absurdity of Betty's statement.

"I'm educating you."

"Funny," said Katherine, although she wasn't the slightest bit amused, "I thought that was my job."

Katherine locked her office door and headed outside. It was the end of a long day. She was tired and feeling out of sorts. Winter was hanging on, she was aching for warmth and bright sunshine, and she hadn't heard from Paul since the night he'd proposed. She'd sent him several letters, and they hadn't been returned, which she interpreted as a hopeful sign. On the other hand, Paul hadn't written or called, which meant he still felt angry and hurt by her rejection.

She didn't regret anything she had done or said that night. She loved Paul. She couldn't imagine a time when she wouldn't love him, no matter what the circumstances of her life. But she wasn't ready to marry him. She suspected she might never be. And in spite of the strong attraction between them, she hadn't wanted to sleep with him. She felt too confused and conflicted.

Nothing had happened between her and Bill, probably nothing ever would. Since that night, they had exchanged only brief hellos while rushing across the campus. He no doubt thought she was engaged. She wasn't about to call him up to tell him otherwise. The explanation was very complicated—so complicated that she didn't understand it herself.

Despite her fatigue, she was happy to see Joan as she stepped out into the chilly air. Of all her students, Joan was her favorite . . . so bright, so eager to learn, one of the few girls she'd encountered at Wellesley who seemed brave enough to take risks.

Joan handed her an envelope. Her name was on the front, written in flawless calligraphic script.

"What's this?" said Katherine, holding the envelope in her palm, as if weighing the contents.

"Every year the ARs nominate a member of the faculty to be our guest," Joan said.

"The what?" Just when she thought she'd learned all the Wellesley customs and traditions, rituals and ceremonies, here was another one that somehow involved her.

"You'll see," Joan said. "The invitation tells you everything you need to know."

Katherine had to show up at seven thirty the following Thursday at an unfamiliar address, just off campus. Joan was waiting for her in front of the small white house. She was dressed in capris, her red senior beanie, and a matching cardigan sweater with AR sewn on the right lapel in bold white letters.

"Adam's Rib," said Joan.

Katherine smiled, but Joan kept a straight face. Katherine got the message: she was supposed to take seriously whatever was about to happen. Joan rapped on the door, using a special configuration of knocks and pauses to signal that she and their guest had arrived.

Connie opened the door. She was wearing a red beanie and cardigan just like Joan's. "First, the oath," she said to Katherine. "Raise both hands."

Katherine thought she was kidding. But the determined look in Connie's eyes told her this was no joke. Katherine raised her hands.

"Do you swear not to repeat what you see, hear, or smell tonight?" said Connie.

"Smell?" Katherine put a hand to her mouth to hide her smile.

"Keep your hands up." Connie sounded like a tough sheriff in a cowboy movie. "Yes, smell."

"I swear," Katherine said solemnly.

"Wait here."

Arms raised and feeling very foolish, Katherine waited outside. After a few seconds, she heard a cacophonous din of chanting and drumming, a Hollywood version of jungle music. Connie opened the door, told Katherine she could lower her arms, and led her into the room.

Katherine recognized the girls—Giselle, Joan, Susan, a few other students she knew less well—all of them wearing beanies and cardigans. The only one missing was Betty. In the middle of the room a large pot filled with bubbling hot liquid was perched unsteadily on a Bunsen burner. A couch, a love seat, and an overstuffed armchair completed the decor.

Giselle scooped up a cup and handed it to Katherine. "It'll only burn a second," she assured her.

Katherine understood that this was a test: Would she agree to drink the brew without asking what was in it? She hesitated only briefly. She'd survived enough fraternity keg parties in college to know her stomach could tolerate almost anything short of rat poison. She put the cup to her mouth and slammed it down in one long gulp.

The girls applauded her performance and helped themselves to the punch, which was obviously well spiked.

"Cheers," Joan said, raising her cup.

Connie emptied a bottle of crème de menthe into the punch. "We're not allowed to have alcohol," she said, stating the obvious.

"We all do things we're not allowed to do,"

said Giselle. "Now that you've taken the oath, we get to ask you whatever we want." She pointed to the armchair, the hot seat for the guest of honor.

"Is that how it works?" Katherine added up the elements: spiked punch, a secret vow, a roomful of curious girls on the verge of womanhood. The ingredients were harmless by themselves, but mix them all together, and she could have the recipe for disaster.

"You have to answer," Susan said, at the same moment that Betty, late as usual, strolled in. "You're just in time for truth or consequences."

Betty wrinkled up her nose, as if she smelled something nasty. She glanced at Katherine. "You must be kidding. Who invited her?"

Betty threw herself down on the couch. Everyone gathered around Katherine.

"I go first," Joan said, asking the question they were all dying to have answered. "Why aren't you married?"

"Hmm." Katherine had no easy answer. "I'm not married," she said, "because . . . I'm not. Things were different before the war. I was engaged to Howie Fox. He was the first person I danced with, smoked with, got drunk with. We shared a lot of firsts."

The girls giggled. They were happy to use

their imaginations to fill in what Katherine left blank.

"We were eighteen and getting married Christmas of forty-one. Then Pearl Harbor happened. And everything that seemed important before didn't matter anymore. By June he was overseas."

"How tragic!" Connie exclaimed. She could see the drama unfolding before her: the handsome young soldier, his beautiful fiancée back home knitting socks and praying for his safe return, and then the inevitable . . .

Joan, the budding law student, wanted to know all the facts. "Did he come back?"

"Yes."

"Was he changed?" asked Susan, creating her own version of the story.

"She was," Giselle said softly.

Everyone, Katherine included, stared at Giselle, who continued. "He expected everything to be the way it was, but she couldn't go back. She didn't know how." She shrugged her shoulders. "My folks were the same. They got divorced. First on my block. And that's a city block."

Now it was Connie's turn. "UCLA's in Hollywood, right?"

"Close."

"Aren't you going to tell everyone about . . . you know . . . your big news?" said Giselle.

"What are you talking about?" Susan asked.

Only the greatest exertion of willpower had kept Giselle from broadcasting the news of Miss Watson's engagement. She had promised herself that she would wait until Katherine showed up wearing her ring so the girls could hear Giselle's version of the story. But here they all were, talking about marriage, and Miss Watson was still pretending nothing had happened. She was just too maddening!

"She got engaged over Christmas," Giselle announced.

The girls looked at Giselle, then at one another. Who got engaged? And why didn't they know about it?

"Sorry to blab, but it was so romantic," Giselle apologized to Katherine. "I ran into them at the Blue Ship," she explained to the other girls. "He's very handsome."

A moment of quiet before the storm of excitement when they realized what Giselle was telling them about Miss Watson. A secret engagement was much more interesting and thrilling than anything they had expected to hear this evening.

Joan was the first to jump up and throw her arms around her favorite teacher. Then Connie was crying for joy and hugging her, and Susan was so excited she couldn't stop screaming. Giselle grabbed a bunch of cups and filled them with punch. Now they really had a lot to toast. Only Betty held back, refusing to join in the celebration, a sour expression on her face.

"He is very handsome," Katherine said, a blush rising in her cheeks. "That's true. And he's also available."

"What?" A chorus of consternation led by Joan, and echoed by the rest.

"Not every relationship is right for marriage." The words sounded pat and evasive, but they were as close to an explanation as Katherine could come up with. How else to explain what she herself didn't understand?

"Like Professor Dunbar," Betty said loudly. "He's strictly an affair, right?" She glared at Katherine, daring her to deny the truth. Miss Watson was a troublemaker. Somebody had to blow the whistle on her, expose her as the subversive that she was.

"What?" Katherine

"You won't be the first," Betty said.

"Shut up!" said Giselle, who also didn't like where the conversation was going.

Betty pointed to Katherine. "She's the one who's encouraged us to speak out. You don't believe in holding back, do you, Miss Watson?"

"No," Katherine said. "I do, however, believe in good manners. But for you, I'll make an exception. That's what we're supposed to do for married students, right, Betty? No. I'm not having an affair with Professor Dunbar. Next?"

"Did you have one with William Holden?" Connie asked.

"Connie!" Joan scolded.

"What?" Connie jerked her head toward Betty. "*She* asked about Bill Dunbar."

Katherine was blushing. "I cannot believe that followed me across the country," she said, laughing weakly.

Connie jumped on her comment as an admission. "Oh, it's true!"

The girls laughed and applauded. Betty, however, wasn't amused. "Won't you regret never marrying?" she said, zeroing in on what she assumed was her teacher's weak spot.

"There's still time," Joan said hopefully.

Katherine laughed. "I hope and assume I'll get married. I'm just not going to plan my life around it."

"And neither should we?" Betty's voice dripped sarcasm.

Katherine was astonished by her hostility. "I never said that."

"Well, you did to Joan. At least that's what she told me."

"What are you saying?" Joan glared at her

friend, baffled by the direction Betty was taking the conversation.

"She knew you and Tommy were seconds away from engagement. And still she practically filled out your law school application."

"I didn't say that," Joan snapped.

"You applied to law school?" Susan sounded as incredulous as if Joan had just announced she was running for president of the United States.

"She's been accepted," Betty said.

"Betty!" Joan scowled at Betty. She had sworn her to secrecy, and yet Betty had so carelessly, gleefully, betrayed her trust.

"You got in?" Katherine said.

"Now she just has to figure out a way to tell Tommy," Betty said spitefully.

Katherine was so angry that she couldn't stop herself from speaking her mind. "Why don't you do it for her, Betty? You seem so good at butting into other people's business."

"Funny," Betty sneered. "That's what they say about you."

"Do they?" Katherine managed a halfhearted laugh, but Betty's gibe stung.

From the very first day, Betty had adamantly resisted Katherine's belief that there was more to life after graduation than marriage and babies. Katherine felt sorry for the girl: she was so programmed to follow her mother's model that she was incapable of finding her own way. But she could be cruel and dangerous, too. Her damning article about Amanda had cost the nurse her job.

Betty was in some ways a barometer of the times. The country was at war with itself. In Washington, Joe McCarthy was finding Communists behind every tree and screaming for their heads. Katherine had seen for herself the havoc McCarthy and his flunkies had created in Los Angeles, where well-respected actors were waiting tables, and experienced screenwriters had to use pseudonyms to sell their scripts.

All it took these days to wreck a life was for someone to point an accusing finger. Betty seemed to be setting up Katherine as her next target. Katherine wanted to leave Wellesley on her own terms, not because somebody disagreed with her ideas or thought she dispensed too much advice.

But what if—and Katherine had to force herself to contemplate this possibility—there was some truth in Betty's accusation? Did she interfere too much in her students' lives? And might it also be true that other people—people Katherine respected and liked—agreed with Betty that she was getting too involved?

She looked around at the girls, who were eagerly anticipating her response. She saw in their faces so much promise, if only they had the courage to embrace the possibilities. But their only goal was a ring on their finger and a husband who could make their dreams come true. She drained her cup of punch and stood up to leave. Beware of what you wish for, she thought. The line between a dream and a nightmare was often as thin as an acrobat's tightrope.

As editor-in-chief of *The Daily Wellesley*, Betty had almost free rein over the editorial content, and the features editor happened to be one of her dearest friends. So it didn't take much for Betty to sell Gigi on an article about the charms of married life, using Betty and Spencer as the focal point of the piece. Gigi and Betty agreed that because they were such a cute couple, someone should go over to take photographs, black-and-white evidence that Wellesley students could have it all: a first-class education and a traditional, happy marriage.

Betty dressed up for the occasion: a sky blue full-skirted dress with a tightly cinched belt and a Peter Pan collar, pearls, of course, nylon stockings and black pumps, manicured nails with clear polish, and as the final touch, a frilly apron that Susan had given her at her kitchen shower. The apron was more than just a prop. She had decided to make a chicken while Louise, the paper's photographer, was taking pictures, in order to make the story feel really authentic. The Spencer Joneses at home. A chicken in the pot, a book in Betty's hand.

Louise was a junior, and she knew Betty from working with her on the newspaper. Betty started by giving her a tour of the house, and Louise was so impressed that she almost ran out of flattering adjectives. She gasped and cooed over the dining room set that seated twelve with the cunning extensions, the floral-patterned matching couch and love seat in the living room, the green chenille bedspread, and even the shower curtain in the bathroom.

"You look beautiful," she told Betty, looking at her through the viewfinder of her camera.

Betty smiled. If only Spencer was behaving a teensy bit more welcoming and interested. He hadn't been thrilled with the idea in the first place, but now that Louise was here, Betty expected her husband to put on his best face. For heaven's sake, she was all dressed up and he didn't even seem to notice.

"Spencer?" she prompted him. "Do I look all right?"

Spencer was slouched in a chair, drinking a Scotch and checking the sports page to see whether the Red Sox had finally won a game. He gave Betty the briefest glance and said,

"Yeah, fine. I don't have a lot of time here. Can we speed things up?"

"Mr. Grouchy!" she said. She smiled to show she was just kidding because she knew how busy he was. She wanted to say, *Please, honey, just this once, do what I ask.* But she knew that pleading with him didn't help, and it wasn't the sort of thing you could say in front of someone else. So she put her hand on his shoulder, picked up a spoon to stir the pot, and said, "Go ahead, Louise."

The article caused a sensation. The pictures balanced the text, which Betty wrote herself. A photo of Betty at the ironing board with a book lying open next to Spencer's shirt, and Spencer reading in the background, was a perfect illustration for the opening paragraph:

> Wellesley girls who are married have become quite adept at balancing obligations. One hears comments such as, "I'm able to baste the chicken with one hand and outline the paper with the other."

Another picture showed Betty pushing a vacuum with one hand, holding a textbook in the other, and Spencer sitting behind her, smoking his pipe. Here the article read:

> The young married set agrees that BAs and MRSs are as good a combination as Jensen silver and Lowey china. As seniors our perspective is unique. While our mothers were called to the workforce for Lady Liberty, it is our duty, nay obligation, to reclaim our place in the home, bearing the children that will carry our traditions into the future.

Katherine was in her office, drinking her second cup of coffee when she discovered the article on the front page of the paper. She read the first paragraph and looked at the byline: BETTY WARREN. No surprise. Betty was a very good writer. She had been asked to apply to be a guest editor at *Mademoiselle,* to work on the magazine's annual college issue. Only twenty college students from across the country were accepted each summer. But Betty wouldn't even consider the coveted internship because, she had told her faculty adviser, "I would rather die than be apart from Spencer for two months."

Poor Betty. She was too thoroughly brainwashed even to consider other options. The second paragraph had Katherine shaking her head in disgust. The words sounded so much like Betty's mother that they could have come straight from her mouth. She read farther. And then it got personal:

> And so one must pause to consider why Miss Katherine Watson, instructor in the art history department, has decided to declare war on the holy sacrament of marriage. Her subversive and political teachings encourage our Wellesley girls to reject the roles they were born to fill.

Katherine's hands were suddenly shaking. She was so furious that she didn't feel the hot coffee spill onto her lap and soak through her skirt onto her bare legs. She was so angry that she couldn't imagine walking into the lecture hall to teach her class. She had come east with an open mind and heart, but now she felt out of her element. To be fair, although most of the students she'd met at Wellesley were content to follow the rules, Betty was the only girl who thought spiteful was a synonym for bright and savvy. But how could Katherine give a lecture on Rembrandt and portraiture when she was too hurt and angry to remember why she loved teaching?

She decided to send a message that class was canceled for the day because she was ill. She had her hand on the phone to call Dr. Staunton's secretary when a much better solution took shape in her mind. She quickly dug through her slides and found the set she'd used for a women's club lecture about the use of imagery in advertising. There was more than one way to skin a cat, her mother used to say. It was a stupid expression, one which always irritated Katherine, but meaningful now that she had an unruly, sharp-nailed cat clawing at her.

Katherine walked into the lecture hall just in time to see Giselle throwing the paper onto Betty's desk and irately demanding, "Who died and made you God?"

Katherine silently set up the slides, ignoring the girls' inquiring glances.

"Lights," she said.

The first slide was a newspaper advertisement that featured a flustered woman. The text beneath the illustration read: COULD YOU GET A JOB AS A HOUSEWIFE? USE AJAX CLEANSER!

"Contemporary art," said Katherine.

"But that's just an advertisement," Connie called out.

Katherine cut her off. "Quiet. Today, you just listen."

She got a perverse pleasure from the girls' stunned silence.

"What will future scholars see when they study us?" asked Katherine. "The portraits of women today? There you are, ladies. The perfect likeness of a Wellesley graduate. Magna cum laude. Doing exactly what she was trained to do."

She moved on to the next slide, this one a picture of a thirtyish woman, her face slathered with cold cream. And the text: LUX ONE-MINUTE MASK. SHOW HIM A NEW FACE EVERY DAY!

"Oh, look! A Rhodes scholar. I wonder if she recites Chaucer while she's applying her cold cream," Katherine commented.

Click! Slide three: A young woman in her brand-new kitchen, wearing a spotless polka-dot apron, proudly holding up a pan of meat loaf. The text here read: PLAIN DISH. PLAIN LOVE. SPICE YOUR LIFE WITH DEL MONTE CATSUP!"

"And you physics majors can calculate the mass and volume of every meat loaf you make," said Katherine.

She moved on to the next slide, yet another ad, this one showing yet another young woman with a model-thin figure wearing a housedress. YOU COULDN'T CHOOSE A BETTER WAY TO BE FREE! ELASTIC GIRDLE!

"A girdle to set you free? What does that mean?" Katherine almost shouted at the girls.

She had more such slides, but she couldn't stand to look at another one.

"I give up!" she said, pacing the aisle. "You win. The smartest women in the country? I never realized that by demanding excellence, I'd be challenging . . . what did it say? 'The roles you were born to fill.' Forgive me for expecting so much."

She fell silent, her face a rigid mask of anger and disappointment. "Class dismissed," she said finally, and then she marched out of the room, leaving the girls so taken aback that not one of them, not even Betty, could think of anything to say.

"I quit," Katherine announced to President Carr. "I'm not putting on a girdle to be free."

She had burst into the president's office without as much as a knock on the door.

President Carr stared at her in disbelief. "You're not what?"

"And you're not going to change my mind," Katherine declared.

President Carr sighed loudly. "I assume this has something to do with today's editorial." She motioned for Katherine to sit down.

"It has more to do with the school. Look at your girls, President Carr. Aren't you proud?" said Katherine, seating herself on the edge of the chair.

"Yes, actually, I am," said the president.

"You should be," Katherine said, not bothering to hide her scorn. "Half of them are married, and the rest . . . what? Give it a month or so? That's the reason they're really here, right? Just biding time until someone asks?"

"A hundred years ago, it was inconceivable for a woman to be a college graduate. Perhaps you should look back to see how far we've come," President Carr said calmly.

She shook her head. "Sorry, but from where I sit, it's just a different kind of corset."

"We all need a little support," President Carr said, smiling in a futile attempt to defuse the tension.

Katherine ignored her. "The kind you gave Amanda Armstrong?"

"She broke the law," President Carr calmly reminded her.

"According to Betty Warren," Katherine said.

"According to the State of Massachusetts."

Katherine stood up. The discussion was headed nowhere that might be useful. At this point, she had only one choice. "I resign," she said.

"I won't let you," said President Carr, no longer smiling.

"I'm not asking permission. Besides, we all know who runs the place. It's only a matter of time before Betty gets me fired, too," Katherine said.

"Well, until then, you have a contract," the president pointed out. "I suggest you uphold it."

Her words rang in Katherine's ears as she left

the room. No matter. She might as well start packing now because with Betty Warren and her mother lined up against her, Katherine would be out of a job in the time it took the average Del Monte housewife to whip up a meat loaf.

She didn't know where to go, whom to turn to for encouragement. Nancy would never understand. Paul might, but things felt too messy between them right now to call him up and cry about a choice he had never supported. She hurried down the hall, hoping to hold back her tears until she could cry in private. Glancing through a classroom window, she saw Bill sitting at his desk, reading. Without thinking, she rushed into the room. "Screw Wellesley. I'm done," she said.

He stared at her in astonishment, as did the roomful of his students busy taking a test.

She slapped her forehead. "Sorry," she said to the girls, whom she hadn't even noticed. "God, it just keeps getting worse." Shaken and embarrassed, she hurried out of the room,

Bill turned to his class and said, "*Momento,*" then quickly followed her.

"Think about it. It's brilliant," Katherine said, starting the conversation in midthought. "A perfect ruse. A finishing school disguised as a college. They got me."

"What did you expect?" Bill said, not unsympathetically.

"More," she admitted, fighting back tears. "I thought I was headed to the place that would turn out tomorrow's leaders, not their wives. Everyone is afraid here. Even you, with your language program, right? You didn't want to risk tenure?" She glared at him, as if he, too, were the enemy.

A group of girls passed by, whispering and giggling as they openly stared at the two professors, who looked as if they were having a lovers' quarrel.

"Can you keep it down please?" Bill hissed. "I have ten more minutes here. Meet me in my office downstairs."

Katherine desperately needed to be alone. She said, "No, I—"

He cut her off. "I said, meet me."

When he put it that way, she had no choice.

She hadn't seen Bill's office before. It was decorated, if that was the word, with memorabilia of Italy: pictures; a tiny reproduction of the Duomo; a map of Italy with colored pins marking various spots, presumably cities and towns where Bill had fought or visited; and photos of Bill in uniform, a few of him alone, more of him with his buddies.

He pointed to the picture that Katherine was

holding. "That's me and Stan in San Remo. The whole village was wiped out two days later." He took it out of her hand and put it back on the shelf. "How are you feeling?"

She mustered up a weak smile. "Stupid. Deceived. Angry. Shall I go on?"

"Change, especially the kind you want to make, takes time," said Bill. He sat down on his cluttered desk and offered her a jelly bean from the jar next to the telephone. Katherine shook her head. It would take more than sugar to improve her mood.

Bill popped a handful into his mouth. "Give them a chance to catch up. They need you here, Katherine. We all do. How they let you in beats the hell out of me. But I'm sure glad they did," he said.

Katherine sat down and leaned back into the chair. Now that she was calmer, she was beginning to feel more than a little foolish about barging into the president's office. "The things I said to President Carr, she'll never ask me back," she said, grimacing as she replayed the conversation in her head.

"She's a pretty good egg."

Katherine rolled her eyes.

"What things?" he said, trying to gauge how far she had taken her indignation. Then, fish-ing for information, he added, "Unless you want to get back to California, and that fiancé of yours."

"We're not engaged. Don't ask," Katherine muttered. She picked up her coat and scarf and headed for the door. "Sorry about all this."

Bill couldn't help her. Nobody could. She had created her own mess, and it was up to her to clean it up.

She took a walk around the lake. The weather was cold, verging on bitter, and her teeth chattered in spite of all the warm layers she wore. But she needed to be outside, somewhere that wasn't cluttered with the trappings of her past and present. The wind was blowing directly in her face, and she wasn't sure whether her tears were from the chill or her feelings of regret, disappointment, and failure.

She had been walking for almost half an hour when she thought she heard a voice calling her name. She turned around and saw Bill just a few yards away, cupping his hands to his mouth. "Katherine!" he called out again.

She stopped to let him catch up. He handed her a package, wrapped in paper that was decorated with Christmas trees.

"Sorry about the wrapping," he said. "It was

going to be for Christmas. Then I met him and . . ." He grinned sheepishly. "Open it. Go on."

It was a 3-D slide viewer, along with a package of slides. She looked at him and he nodded. She inserted one after another, with Bill providing a running commentary.

"The Sistine Chapel. *The David. Venus de Milo.*"

She began to cry for no reason she could think of, other than Bill's kindness. When he leaned over to kiss her, she almost kissed him back. Remembering all the gossip she'd heard, she pulled away just as their lips were about to meet.

"I'm sorry," he said, red faced. "I didn't mean to . . ."

"I'm not one of your students," she said, staring at the ice-covered lake.

"There's just been one, you know. Student."

She turned to face him. In a tone that came out far harsher than she'd meant it to, she said, "Well, that's one too many."

Connie was having the kind of day that felt too much fun to be real. She almost had to keep pinching herself to make sure she wasn't dreaming. She had always loved Cape Cod, the arm-shaped peninsula that jutted into the Atlantic a couple of hours from Boston. But she'd only been there in the summer when the beaches were crowded with vacationing families, and the aroma from the lobster joints was too enticing to pass up. She would never have expected to find herself there on a cold gray Saturday in February. Charlie knew a neat little hotel in Hyannis. Would she like to take a drive and do something different? They could leave first thing in the morning, spend the day, and have dinner at one of his favorite restaurants.

She hesitated a second before saying yes. She knew what he was really asking her, and she still wasn't quite sure how he felt about her. But she wanted to be with him so badly that she sometimes sat in her room all day, waiting for him to call. So she said yes, and by the time they crossed the Bourne Bridge, which linked the Cape to the mainland, she had made up her mind to go as far as he wanted.

The hotel that Charlie took her to looked out onto the water, and the place was just shabby enough to feel comfortable. He lit a fire in the room's fireplace and offered her a Bloody Mary. Before they were halfway through their drinks, he put his arm around her, and kissed her harder and longer than she'd ever been kissed before. Soon after that, they found their way to his bedroom, quickly pulled off their clothes, and huddled under the quilt for warmth. And so the day passed. The ham-and-cheese sandwiches, potato chips, and brownies that she'd brought for lunch never got eaten.

They finally disentangled themselves in the late afternoon and walked out onto the dunes. The tide was low, and the waves lapped gently at the sand. Connie took off her stockings and high heels and played surf tag, a game from her childhood, jumping over the incoming waves before the water could reach her ankles. Charlie went searching for seashells, but he soon gave up and joined her at the water's edge. She giggled because he looked so silly and dear, dressed up in a dark woolen suit jacket and tie, his shoes dangling around his neck and his suit pants rolled up to his knees.

She was suddenly ten years old again and playing on the beach with Tommy, her summer next-door neighbor whom she'd adored for as long as she could remember. They had spent countless days together on the beach, building sand castles, digging to China, diving for clamshells, splashing each other until they were both soaking wet. She hadn't seen Tommy in years, but the game still seemed like fun. She grabbed Charlie's arm and pulled him far enough into the surf that his pants were quickly soaked way past his knees. The water was icy cold. Charlie's first reaction was a howl of indignation, and then he came after her, spraying her mercilessly until they were both soaking wet and breathless with laughter.

They raced back to the car, turned the heater on high, and dried themselves off as best they could. By then, the sun was setting and they couldn't wait for dinner. The restaurant where Charlie had made reservations was in Hyannis proper, a rambling old building that had formerly been a private home. It had a long oak bar in one room, and lots of smaller rooms decorated with paintings of sea captains and what purported to be their boats.

"Starving?" Charlie said as they waited for the hostess to seat them.

"Famished. And please don't say we can live on love. That's how I missed breakfast and lunch," said Connie, squeezing his arm as she thought about his face next to hers on the pillow, her head in the crook of his arm.

Charlie winked at her and smiled, and then his smile suddenly faded.

"What's the matter?" she said.

She followed his gaze and saw an older couple across the room.

"Phillip and Vanessa McIntyre. Parents of a friend," he said.

"Do you want to say a quick hello?"

He shook his head and scowled. "No, I'll be trapped. Damn."

Connie thought she understood. This day was so special, just for the two of them. Their romantic dinner for two could be ruined if they ended up with a table for four.

"I have an idea," she told Charlie, as the hostess approached them. Connie smiled sweetly and said, "Could you seat us in the bar?"

"I'm sorry," said the hostess. "We're only serving in the front part of the restaurant this evening."

Connie was determined to have her way, if only to show Charlie how much his happiness meant to her. Signaling the hostess that she needed to speak with her in private, she moved closer to the bar and read the woman's name tag.

"Listen, Miss Stone," she said. "This has been the most romantic weekend I may ever have, and all that stands between right now and perfection are the McIntyres over there, who for whatever reason my boyfriend doesn't want to see. Now you know as well as I, with the competition out there, a girl has to be able to move a few mountains once in a while. I could use all the help I can get. What do you say? Please?"

The hostess nodded. Connie didn't have to say another word. She completely understood. Women had to look out for each other. "Right this way," she said. Picking up two menus, she led Connie and Charlie to the bar.

The look on Charlie's face was all the thanks Connie needed. He was impressed with her, and maybe even in love.

Chapter Eight

Synchronized swimming with Miss Albini was a Wellesley rite of passage. No one remembered how sync swim, as it was commonly known, had come to be part of the physical education program. Perhaps a wealthy alumna had admired Esther Williams or Busby Berkeley's choreographed water extravaganzas from the 1930s Warner Brothers movies. But the sport, if it could be called such, was an important part of the athletic department. Students were required to take at least five semesters of physical ed, so girls who hated sports, but didn't mind swimming, took Miss Albini's class. Girls who couldn't swim, but weren't jocks, fulfilled their phys ed requirement with duckpin bowling.

Betty, Giselle, and their crowd had opted for

sync swim. They spent more time out of the pool than in it by telling Miss Albini that their "friend" was visiting, which meant they were having their period. The real fun was sitting at poolside, watching Miss Albini as she instructed their more conscientious classmates to dip and flutter, kick and turn, breathe and smile, in time to dippy songs like Doris Day's "By the Light of the Silvery Moon."

The girls were fascinated by Miss Albini, in the same way that people were so mesmerized by the sight of a horrible car crash that they had to stop and stare at the injured, bloodied victims. Although none of them would admit it, Miss Albini scared them. She was in her late thirties but looked older; she was extremely prim and proper and was fastidious about her appearance and wore her hair in a low chignon. The only time she changed out of her starched white shirts and long dark skirts was to teach swimming, in which case she wore a baggy black bathing suit that was a throwback to the 1940s. Like Nancy Abbey, she was a Wellesley graduate who had never married, never left the campus. But Miss Abbey at least was still making an effort to wear an up-to-date hairstyle and fashionable clothes. She was *old,* but she didn't scream *old maid,* which poor Miss Albini definitely did.

"She's much too happy," Giselle said, watching Miss Albini enthusiastically rehearse her students.

The girls nodded. They'd had this same conversation before, and they had yet to figure out the source of Miss Albini's apparent contentment with her life.

Connie pulled herself to her feet and said, "I have biology. See you later."

Betty had been unusually quiet throughout the class, and when Joan had asked if she was okay, she'd said, yes, of course, peachy. But she seemed gloomy and, most telling of all, hadn't made a single nasty crack about anyone. Now she said, "How about we all have lunch on Saturday? Just us girls."

"I'm busy," Giselle said.

"I'm free," Susan said.

"What are you doing?" Joan asked Giselle.

"She's dating a psychoanalyst," said Connie as she grabbed her towel and cigarettes.

"Really?" Joan hadn't heard this latest development.

"Who's married." Giselle bit her lip. "Sorry, it slipped."

"Giselle!" Joan scolded.

Giselle shrugged. "I'm not ashamed. We're just in it for the sex."

"Spare us," said Betty, rolling her eyes at Joan. "Connie? You in?"

Connie suddenly got very absorbed in folding her towel. "I'll have to check with Charlie," she said.

"Who?" Betty wanted to know.

"Charlie Stewart," said Giselle. "You remember. *Your* Charlie. Now he's *hers*."

Betty stared at Connie, not bothering to hide her amazement. "You're kidding!" she exclaimed.

"We spent last weekend at the Cape," said Connie. "A little hideaway he knew about."

"Operative word, *hide*," Betty said, sounding more like her old self. "Men take women to the Cape in the winter when they're embarrassed to be seen with them. He's using you."

"He's not using her if she wants to go," Giselle informed Betty. She turned to Connie and said, "Don't listen."

Betty reached over and put her hand on Connie's arm. "Connie, I love you. I swear I'm not saying this to hurt you. But Charlie Stewart is promised to Deb McIntyre. She wears his pin. And, Giselle, you know it's true."

"I don't know about the pin," Giselle said, lighting up a cigarette.

Confused and upset, Connie zeroed in on something Betty had just said. "McIntyre? Are her parents Phillip and Vanessa?"

"Good God! You know them?" said Betty.

Connie's face had turned pale, and she looked

as if she were about to be sick. "Only from a distance," she said. She grabbed her towel and strode away from the pool area without even bothering to say good-bye. The rest of the girls looked at one another: Now what was that all about?

Katherine had just finished paying for the new paperback edition of Edna Ferber's *Giant* at the campus bookstore when she bumped into Joan, who was buying a copy of *Great Expectations* for her English literature course. As they left the store together, Katherine asked, "What does Tommy think about this whole law school thing?" Katherine was pleased to have these few minutes alone with Joan. She had been meaning to ask her about Tommy's reaction to Joan's postgraduation plan, which she sensed might be a touchy subject, but this seemed like the perfect opportunity.

"I can't tell." Joan sounded unconcerned. "I mean, he's really encouraging. It's just that everything is happening all at once."

Katherine wasn't convinced by Joan's offhand tone. She hoped that Tommy was in fact as accepting as Joan was making him out to be. "He'll get used to the idea," she said reassuringly.

"I'm not worried," said Joan. She checked her watch. "Yikes! I'm about to miss the train.

Thanks again, Miss Watson," she called over her shoulder as she took off running.

Katherine was still pondering Joan's casual approach to her future when she heard a loud honking and someone calling her name.

"Katherine?" She turned around and saw Bill's car.

He quickly pulled up at the curb and jumped out of the car. "Katherine," he said, "I've been looking for you."

She smiled at him. He looked as elated as a small boy with a new baseball glove. "You found me. Is everything all right?"

He was almost twitching with excitement. "Better than that. Everything's great! They said yes to my language program. I gave it another shot, and what do you know?"

It took her a moment to understand what he was talking about; then she broke into a huge grin. No wonder he was so thrilled! "What do you know?" she said, sharing his pleasure.

"Well, I just wanted to say thanks." He was holding his car keys, and now he nervously tossed them from one hand to the other. "If it weren't for you, I might not have tried. So thanks," he said again, sounding ill at ease.

They hadn't spoken, except for a brief hello when they happened to cross paths, since the day at the lake, when he had kissed her. She'd wondered when he was going to call, and when he didn't, she could have kicked herself for having so rudely dismissed him. Here was the perfect opportunity to make it up to him.

"Can a gal buy you a drink to celebrate?" she said.

He smiled. "Sure thing." But when she walked around to the driver's side of the car, he looked alarmed. "Where are you going?"

She'd missed driving, and she'd been dying to get behind the wheel of Bill's car since the first time she'd seen it. Acting on an impulse, she said, "Hop in, hot rod. You're not the only one who can drive, you know."

She liked being in the driver's seat, especially in an Alfa Romeo, which picked up faster and hugged the road more smoothly than any car she'd ever owned. She was going over the speed limit, but the car felt as if it were driving itself, and she was having too much fun to put on the brakes.

Drinks led to dinner at a small Italian restaurant, run by Mauro and Graziella, a married couple who greeted Bill like an old friend and brought them a series of dishes that weren't on the menu. While they chatted with one another in Italian, Katherine smiled and happily ate the mouthwatering food that kept appearing at the table. She hadn't realized until now how much she missed this experience: sharing a delicious meal and interesting conversation with an attractive man who obviously enjoyed her company. Bill had a way of looking at her that made her feel beautiful, that made her want to lean over and kiss him.

She didn't want the evening to end. When they left the restaurant, after lingering over tiny cups of espresso, Paul suggested a nightcap at his house. She said yes without a moment's hesitation, even though they both knew what would happen if she went to his place instead of going straight home.

As they sat in his living room, drinking brandy, they talked about everything except the topic that was uppermost in both their minds. Then they stopped talking and moved into each other's arms, as easily as if they had planned all along to spend the night together. Her first thought was that she was kissing a man, and he wasn't Paul. Then she stopped thinking and simply gave herself up to the experience, which was simultaneously the same and very different from anything she had done in the past.

Afterward, she could not have said how they ended up in his bedroom, hastily undressing, finding their way together. She could not have said how this man, whom she knew so little about, seemed so familiar, so loving and generous in how he made love with her.

At some point in the night, so late that it was already early morning, the house got very cold. They went downstairs so Bill could rebuild the fire in the living room. Katherine sat on the sofa, staring out his window, which overlooked Lake Waban. The first glimmering of light was showing in the sky. She had hardly slept, but she felt too happy and content to be tired. She had an impulse to get up and put her arms around Bill, as he knelt at the fireplace, but he suddenly turned around and said, sounding almost angry, "I don't know how I feel about being a rebound."

She was so taken aback that all she could do was nod, get up from the sofa, and say, "I'll leave."

With one quick step, he was standing next to her, shaking his head, hugging her. "No, I'm okay with it, honestly," he said, his mouth against her hair. "What are you doing?"

"Getting dressed," she said, hoping she sounded more confident and lighthearted than she felt. "Listen, I had fun, and I'm not looking for anything serious here."

"Come back under the covers," he said, tracing his fingers down her back. "We'll discuss it."

She instantly forgave him. She might have felt the same had she met the woman who was supposed to be his fiancée, which made her realize she needed to set some ground rules. "As long as we're doing whatever it is we're doing . . ."

He grinned and pushed her down onto the sofa. "Which we did pretty well—don't you think?"

"No students," she said sternly, moving out of his reach. "I mean it. I don't want to stand in class and wonder why the girl in the third row is wearing my perfume."

"Katherine, I—"

"I need your word," she insisted.

He put up his right hand. "All right. You have my word." He pulled her back into his arms and said, "Can we change the subject now to something more important?"

She nodded, thinking that he wanted to talk about Paul.

"Breakfast," he said. "I make a mean blueberry pancake."

Katherine burst out laughing. "I don't know you well enough for breakfast," she teased.

"What's a fellow have to do to get to know you better?" he asked, gently kissing her neck. "Hmmm. *Bella,* Katarina."

She didn't need an Italian dictionary to know she liked what he was saying. "Getting warmer, definitely," she said. She laid her cheek against his chest and noticed a thin white scar across his belly. Tracing it with her finger, she said, "A battle wound? I'm a sucker for war stories and romance languages."

"In that case," he said, unbuttoning her shirt, "I was in a village called San Remo. The Krauts had pounded us hard."

"Ummmm," she murmured and told him with her fingers to save the rest of the story for later.

Bill screeched to a stop in front of Katherine's house. They had overslept, and they were both late for class, but they couldn't resist one last, long kiss before she got out of the car.

"Good morning," said Bill, finally pulling away from her.

"Good morning," she said, loving the taste of him on her lips.

Bill glanced out the window and saw Nancy peeking through the curtains. He nudged Katherine to follow his gaze. "Looks like we have an audience," she said, smiling.

"In that case . . ." He gathered her into his arms and gave her the kind of intensely lingering kiss that could have been lifted from a Cary Grant romance. Midway through, he raised his hand so that Nancy was sure to see it and made a circle of his thumb and first finger, signaling to her: "A-OK!"

The curtains snapped shut, and her face abruptly disappeared from view.

Katherine hurried inside, hoping to get showered and changed for class without having to listen to Nancy's inevitable sermon. No such luck, alas. Nancy was in the kitchen, her arms crossed against her chest, a pained look on her face.

"Hi, you're up early. Coffee on?" Katherine said breezily.

Nancy got straight to the point. "How could you date a man like that?"

Katherine poured herself a cup of coffee and tried to curb her temper. "What if you're wrong about him? Did you ever consider that?"

"What if I'm not?" Nancy snapped. "Did you?"

Katherine took a sip of coffee and tried to stay calm. She reminded herself that Nancy was trying to be a good friend, even if she was straying far too deeply into Katherine's business. "Coffee's cold," she told Nancy. She spilled the rest of it into the sink. "See you tonight."

The spring formal was held at the end of April, just before reading week and final exams. The girls had talked for weeks of little else. Katherine was hard-pressed to get them to focus on the Post-impressionists when they had urgent decisions to make about the choice of theme and decorations, escorts and gowns. She was relieved when the night of the dance finally arrived—and she was curious, too. She'd never been to a formal. If such an event had been held at UCLA, she certainly had never known about it.

The dance was indeed formal. The girls all wore long white gowns—similar to those worn by the debutantes among them who had come out during their freshman year—and long white gloves. Their escorts were dressed in dinner jackets with bow ties and cummerbunds or suspenders. A few of the men, cadets at West Point, came in their formal military dress. The dance took place in the gymnasium, which was decorated almost beyond recognition with freesias, lilies, and ivy covering all the walls and columns. The lights had been dimmed to cast a romantic glow, and tables covered with white linen cloths had been put up around the perimeter of the dance floor. The huge room resembled a country club dining room, which was exactly the look that the decoration committee had aimed to achieve in keeping with the spring fling theme.

More often than not, the weather cooperated with the scheduling of the dance, and tonight was no exception. The air was soft, the night balmy with just the lightest breeze, so the couples could take a comfortable twilight stroll around the lake.

The entertainment committee had decided that an all-girls school should support an all-girl band, especially since the trumpet and bass players were both alumnae.

"Don't you love girls who play the sax?" said Tommy, as soon as he walked into the gym.

Joan nudged him with her elbow. She wished he didn't always have to play the wiseacre, the guy who just had to come out with the funny line, which sometimes wasn't quite as funny as he thought.

She and Betty had decided to double date. They'd had dinner together and arrived in Tommy's care. Now Spencer turned to Tommy and muttered, "What did you bring?"

Tommy flashed the flask that he had hidden in his jacket pocket. "Dewar's."

Spencer slapped his friend on the back. This party might not be such a drag, after all.

Many of the faculty—including President Carr, Dr. Staunton and other department heads, Nancy, Katherine, and Bill—had turned out to chaperon and just simply enjoy the sight of their girls in a different guise. Nancy had cheerfully volunteered to head up the serving committee.

She loved supervising the presentation of the little sandwiches and other finger foods. Keeping busy meant she didn't feel as conspicuous without a date by her side.

Connie had offered to help Nancy because she didn't have a date, either. Ever since the day at the pool, when Betty had spilled the beans about Charlie and Deb McIntyre, she had avoided his calls until he had stopped calling. She had gloomed around the dorm, trying to put on a brave face, when inside she felt a constant ache in her heart.

Stupid, stupid, stupid, she kept berating herself. She should have known better than to trust a guy like Charlie . . . except that, when she allowed herself to think about him, she kept remembering what a swell time they'd had together. Then the ache would get sharper, and she'd hit the books or do anything to block out the memory of the two of them, in bed together, when all along he was engaged to somebody else.

Susan's advice was just to keep busy, so Connie attached herself to Miss Abbey for the evening. Following her lead, she scurried between the kitchen and the dance floor with trays, pitchers, and whatever else needed replenishing.

"You'd think someone would have noticed

the empty trays," she complained, as she and Nancy lugged several more trays into the gym.

"You're good!" said Nancy. "You remind me of myself when I was your age."

She meant it as a compliment, of course. So why did Connie suddenly want to drop the tray of cookies and run screaming from the building? She had never stopped to imagine Nancy Abbey at her age, a senior at Wellesley, about to go out into the world and discover herself.

What was terrifying—truly, truly terrifying—was that Miss Abbey had not ever found her own place. She was still living in a dormitory of sorts, still on campus, still embracing the traditions, conditions, and mind-set that she had brought with her to college a decade earlier.

Nothing had changed for her. The worst part was that she didn't seem to mind.

Katherine knew she and Bill were causing a stir, and she was taking perverse pleasure in knowing that people were talking about them. They had briefly considered not coming to the dance as a couple, but they had almost immediately dismissed that notion. Why cave in to somebody else's definition of appropriate or seemly instead of doing what felt right to them? They were both adults, unattached, and responsible only to themselves and each other.

* * *

Across the room, Dr. Staunton, who was staring at them, leaned over and whispered something to President Carr.

"Ears burning?" Bill asked Katherine.

"I think the feet go first after they set the stake on fire," she said, laughing.

"Looks like they're talking about you," said Bill. Pitching his voice high, he mimicked President Carr. "What do you say, Edward? Shall we have her back next term?" He lowered his voice and imitated Dr. Staunton: "She has great legs."

Katherine playfully smacked his arm. "Cut it out. What makes you think I want to come back?"

"And leave me here with all these girls?" The band started playing "Sh'Boom" by the Crew Cuts. Bill pulled her onto the dance floor. "Did you know that President Carr and lover boy were once . . . ?"

She burst out laughing as he swung her away from him in rhythm to the music. People looked their way, wondering what the joke was.

"Quiet. Be careful," he said.

"If I were more careful, I wouldn't be here with you," she said and snuggled up against him.

Connie and Giselle, who was also dateless, were watching from the sidelines. Giselle pulled out of her evening bag a small pearl-covered flask. "Cheers!" she said. A sour look on her face, she drank from her private stash of gin.

"It's positively vomitous!" Connie said.

"It's disgusting," Giselle said, glaring at Bill. "I look at him, and I have absolutely no feelings. Want a drink?"

"No, thanks," Connie said.

Giselle went off to the bar in search of more gin. Connie glanced around the room, watching the couples dip and sway. Betty waved from the dance floor, and Connie waved back. She tried to smother a yawn. It was getting late, and she was tired and bored. The thought of toting one more tray of food was too appalling, so she decided to make a quiet exit and go back to the dorm. She turned to leave and there, no more than six feet away, was Charlie Stewart.

Her knees went weak with longing for him. Charlie . . . His arm was draped around a beautiful girl whom Connie didn't recognize, and he was laughing at something the girl had just said. She remembered the sound of his laugh and the feeling of his arm around her shoulder. She wanted to run away, disappear, do anything to avoid him. Before she could move, he looked up, saw her, and smiled.

She watched him say something to his date,

and then he was walking over to her. She took a deep breath and forced herself to smile back at him, although her lips felt unrelated to the rest of her face.

"Connie?" He put a question mark at the end of her name, almost as if he couldn't quite believe she was standing there.

"Charlie," she said, trying to keep her voice from shaking. "It's been a while."

"It has," he said. "How are you?"

Was it just wishful thinking that made her hear discomfort in his voice? She hoped his conscience was bothering him for using her and cheating on his fiancée. Stretching her lips into an even wider smile, she said, "I'm well, thanks. How are you and Debbie?"

It wasn't easy, saying her name out loud, but Connie was glad to have his secret out in the open. She wanted him to know how much he had hurt her.

"Debbie?" Now he sounded confused.

"Your girlfriend with the big teeth." Connie pointed to his date. "Didn't you think I knew?"

She was taken aback by what she read in his eyes—a mixture of pity and regret.

He shook his head, hesitated, then said, "Deb and I broke up last summer. That's Miranda. We met right around the time you stopped taking my calls."

Connie stared at him, too shocked to speak. *Miranda? What was he saying? What about Deb? Betty had told her . . .*

"See you," he said. He returned to Miranda's side before she could manage to eke out a single syllable in response.

The tears started coming so fast that she could hardly find her way as she ran through the crowd. She had to get outside, be alone, away from her friends, teachers, all the people who thought they knew who she was. She had to find someplace private she could cry her heart out until all the tears were spent and she could catch her breath.

She hurried in the direction of the lake, where she knew of several spots shielded from view by the trees. She heard someone yelling her name and pretended not to hear, until she realized it was Betty calling out to her, "Have you seen Spencer?"

She stopped and wiped her eyes before she turned to face her friend. "No," she said, hearing the tremor of rage in her own voice. "But I did see Charlie Stewart. He said he and Deb broke up last summer."

Betty was too busy trying to find her husband to notice her friend's tearstained cheeks and accusing tone. "Yeah?" she said, searching the expanse of lawn between the lake and the gym.

Connie stared at Betty, forcing the other girl to meet her gaze. "You told me he was with her when he invited me to the Cape."

"I what?" Betty said, her eyes darting off again toward the lake. "Oh, come on, Connie. I don't keep track of his dates. They've been on again and off again for the last few years. What don't you understand?"

"Apparently, they've been off again for quite a while."

Betty shrugged. "So?"

"So you made me think he was hiding me."

"How do you know he wasn't?" Betty taunted her.

"It never would have occurred to me either way." Connie was so angry she wanted haul off and smack Betty's face. What would that accomplish, except to give Betty the satisfaction of one more nasty piece of gossip to spread?

Connie really had only herself to blame, for not trusting her own feelings instead of listening to Betty, who was notorious for making trouble. Maybe someday, Betty would get back a taste of her own poison. Maybe she would spend the rest of the evening looking for Spencer and never find him. That would serve her right. Then let her come crying to Connie for sympathy. Fat chance she would ever listen to her again.

"Why couldn't you just let me be happy?" Connie said. She quickly walked away rather than give Betty the satisfaction of having the last word.

What was left to say? Connie's life was ruined. There was nothing for her to do but give up and turn into another pathetic old maid, just like Miss Albini and Miss Abbey.

A switch dance was in progress. Every few minutes the bandleader announced, "And we switch."

Katherine started out with Bill, then found herself with Tommy, while Bill ended up with Nancy.

Tommy twirled her under his arm and grinned. "Wonder Teacher?"

"Tommy Donegal." Katherine could see why Joan was so gone on him. "How's Harvard?"

"Not too bad. Congratulate me," he said, bending her back so low her head almost touched the floor.

She came back into his arms, laughing and breathless. "You set the date?"

"We're talking, but nothing's official yet. I meant that I got into Penn Graduate School."

Joan hadn't told her that Tommy had applied to Penn. Philadelphia was a long way from New Haven. "What about Yale?" she asked.

"Yale? Oh, you mean Joanie. Yeah, how about that? She's some girl, huh?" he said proudly.

"Terrific."

"Just the fact that she got in . . . she'll always have that," he said. "Thanks to you, Miss Watson. You've been swell. It means a lot to both of us."

The music was still playing, but Katherine stopped dancing. "Just the fact that she got in? What does that mean?"

He grabbed her waist and got her moving again. "She'll be with me in Philadelphia."

He didn't say, *of course,* but she knew that's what he meant.

"It's a long commute to get dinner on the table by five o'clock," he said jokingly.

"And we switch," called the bandleader.

Katherine suddenly found herself in the arms of some young man she'd never met. She smiled mechanically and managed to follow his lead. Just like Joan was doing: following, instead of leading.

Betty was frantic. She had spent the last half hour searching for Spencer, with no success. She hurried back to the gym and found Tommy and Joan. "I can't find Spencer anywhere. Do you know where he is?"

Tommy tugged at his bow tie and offered Betty a cookie. She shook her head. Where was her husband?

An awkward pause. Then Tommy said, "Well,

he asked me to take you home. He had an appointment.''

She stared at him, daring him to stop covering up for Spencer. Then her pride got the best of her and she said, pretending to believe him, ''In New York? He had to take the ten o'clock, right?''

Tommy put his hand on her arm, but she shook him off. She could get home by herself, and she knew exactly where she needed to be tonight.

The bandleader announced another switch. Bill was dismayed to find himself partnered with Giselle.

''You two look good together,'' she said.

There was no need to ask whom she had in mind. ''Thanks,'' he said.

She put one hand on the back of his neck and coyly batted her eyes. ''You're usually not so public with your feelings.''

''I am when I feel something. And we switch.'' He removed her hand and walked off the dance floor to search for Katherine.

Giselle wanted to disappear into a hole. She felt angry with Bill and with herself. Most of all, she felt very much alone.

Chapter Nine

Lucinda Warren could not have been more alarmed when she heard the ring of the front doorbell at her Back Bay home. It was eleven o'clock at night, a time when people in their right minds didn't come calling. A visitor at this hour could only mean trouble. She wished her husband were home, but Clayton was away on business. She had no choice but to throw on her dressing gown and hurry downstairs. Remembering the stories she had heard about late-night robberies, she peeked through the lace curtain that covered the window next to the door. Her concern grew even greater when she saw, standing on the steps of the brownstone, her daughter, Betty.

She quickly opened the heavy oak door. "Honey? What are you doing here?"

Betty was carrying an overnight bag. "I'm staying tonight," she said.

Lucinda knew her daughter better than Betty knew herself. She took in Betty's bedraggled appearance, her red-rimmed eyes. "Spencer won't mind?" she asked.

"Spencer won't notice," Betty said. "He's in New York again. Working."

A look of understanding passed between mother and daughter. If Lucinda Warren hadn't guessed before that Betty and Spencer were having problems, everything became clear in that one word: *again*. But Betty's mother had been raised to believe that men and women were held to different standards. She had tried—and thought she had succeeded—in transmitting that belief to her daughter. She had evidently failed.

"Don't get between a man and his career," she told Betty, not unkindly. "He's working hard for both of you."

Betty frowned. Her mother expected her to be an adult, yet treated her like a child. "Don't lie for him, Mother," she snapped. "He does it so well for himself."

"You're going to turn around and go home, fix your face, and wait for your husband," Lucinda Warren said calmly.

Betty was too stunned to speak. Her own

mother . . . Where was she supposed to go, if not home?

"This is the bargain you made, Elizabeth. We all did," Lucinda said, alluding to a fact of her marriage that she would never dream of admitting aloud.

"You're not going to let me into my own house?" Betty asked, too incredulous to grasp what her mother was saying.

"Spencer's house is your house now," Lucinda said firmly. "Believe me, this is for your own good."

The door slammed shut in Betty's face. She reached out to ring the bell again, but stopped herself. There didn't seem to be any point. *Spencer's house,* her mother had said. *For your own good.*

What did those words actually mean? Why was it Spencer's house, and not Betty's, especially since her parents had given it to them as a wedding gift? Why was it still her mother's right to decide what was for Betty's own good?

Good-bye, Mother, and thank you, she said silently, as she headed down the street to find a cab. Her mother had just given her an invaluable graduation present—the freedom to decide what to do with the rest of her life.

Katherine had done a good deal of exploring around Boston, but this was her first trip to Newton, a pretty little town right next to Wellesley. Joan Brandwyn lived in a rambling yellow-and-brown Victorian house on a quiet, tree-lined street off Commonwealth Avenue. Katherine hadn't bothered calling to make sure Joan was at home. As she paid the taxi driver, she wondered whether she had acted too impulsively. On the other hand, her religion professor at UCLA, who had studied the great Buddhist thinkers, had often quoted to the class one of his favorite lines: "First thought, best thought."

Her first thought, after Tommy had told her that he and Joan were moving to Philadelphia, was that Joan should not—could not—give up her dream of law school. Her second led her to explore Joan's options, and here she was two weeks later with a handful of brochures and a plan.

The air smelled of newly mown grass. Spring had finally arrived, and the weather was every bit as magnificent as Katherine had anticipated. She stood a moment on the Brandwyns' porch, admiring the brightly colored posies and petunias in the flower boxes attached to the porch railing. Then she rang the bell and waited.

Joan opened the door and looked at her with obvious surprise. "Miss Watson?"

In her excitement, Katherine launched right into her campaign to ensure that Joan achieve the future she deserved.

"Seven law schools within forty-five minutes of Philadelphia," she said. "You can study *and* get dinner on the table by five o'clock."

"It's too late," Joan said.

Katherine had thought of that, too. "Some of them accept late admissions."

"Stop for a second," said Joan. "Breathe."

"Sorry. New ideas always make me excited. At first, I was upset. When Tommy told me at the dance that he got accepted to Penn, I thought, 'Oh, God, her fate is sealed. But she's worked so hard. How can she throw it all away?' Then it occurred to me, you didn't have to. You could bake your cake and eat it, too."

Joan smiled and shook her head.

"You could!" Katherine insisted.

"We're married."

"What?"

"We eloped over the weekend," said Joan. "Tommy was petrified of the big deal ceremony, so we did a sort of spur-of-the-moment thing. It was very romantic. Look." She held out her left hand and showed Katherine her gold wedding band.

Katherine took hold of Joan's hand and stared at the ring.

"Beautiful," she said, because it was beautiful—the decision had been made. "Congratulations. You can still use these."

She handed Joan the brochures, but Joan pushed them back at her and shook her head. "No, thank you."

Katherine felt sad for Joan, forced to choose between her dreams. "Oh, all right. Well . . ." What more was there to say? She turned to go.

"It was my choice," Joan said.

Katherine turned back. "What?"

"Not to go. He would have supported it."

"But you don't have to choose," she reminded her.

"No, I had to. I want a home. I want a family. That's not something I'm willing to sacrifice."

Joan was such a smart girl. Yet she could not grasp this one simple truth. "No one's asking you to sacrifice a family for a career, Joan. You can have both. You're giving up an opportunity very few girls ever get."

"You think I'm going to wake up one day and regret not being a lawyer?"

"Maybe."

"Not a fraction as much as I'd regret not having my family, not being there to raise them. Despite what you think, I know exactly what I'm doing. It doesn't make me less smart. It just means I'll be putting everything I am, everything I've learned, into something else."

"Making meat loaf?"

"Which must seem heinous to you."

"I didn't say—"

"Sure, you did." Joan interrupted her. "You always did. You stand in class and tell us to look beyond the image. But you never take the time to look beyond it. To you, a housewife is someone who sold her soul for a center-hall Colonial. She has no depth. She has no intellect. She has no interests." Joan stopped, took a breath, and gave Katherine a look that said, *Please listen to me.*

"You're the one who said I could do anything I wanted," she said, pleading to be understood. "This is what I want. Why can't that be enough?"

Wonderful Town, the hit musical about bohemian life in 1930s Greenwich Village, was the hottest ticket in town. Giselle was mad to see it. Rosalind Russell, making her first appearance on Broadway after years in Hollywood, was a sensation, a Tony shoo-in. Giselle told her father that she and a girlfriend from school wanted to see the show, and he easily came up with two tickets. The story was at least half true—the second ticket was for Michael, her married lover.

She adored Michael. He was so funny and sophisticated, and he made her feel so special, sneaking away from his wife to spend time with her. He said that his wife was a bore and a grouch, that she didn't understand him or make him laugh the way Giselle did anymore. And then, of course, there was the sex . . .

Giselle loved teasing Michael. She came up with the most outrageous statements, he pretended to be shocked, and their little game inevitably led to all sorts of interesting developments.

"Sometimes I think you say things to provoke me," Michael said, as they stood in line at the box office, waiting to pick up their tickets to *Wonderful Town*. "Does your father know you talk that way?"

She wasn't fooled a bit by his stern tone, which was part of their game. "Does your wife know you're here?" she said as she leaned up to kiss him.

Michael kissed her back and turned his attention to getting the tickets. Giselle glanced around and noticed a couple across the street locked in a passionate clinch. There was something familiar about the man, who was facing her. When he pulled away from his companion, she realized it was Spencer.

How exciting! She had no idea that he and Betty were in town. She couldn't wait to introduce them to Michael, maybe invite them for a drink after the theater. Betty would be scandalized, of course, which would only add spice to the evening.

She was about to call out their names when she got a closer look at the girl who just a second ago had been locked in Spencer's embrace. The girl was wiping lipstick from Spencer's cheek with a casually intimate touch that spoke of long-standing familiarity.

They made a pretty picture, two young lovers in the spring twilight. From Giselle's perspective, one piece of the picture was terribly wrong: the girl with Spencer wasn't Betty.

Connie was on a mission, and no one was going to stop her. She hurried into Eliot House and raced up the stairs, taking the steps two at a time.

Unaccustomed to the sight of a female breaching their all-male bastion, the men stared at her. The resident tutor was the only one with the presence of mind to yell, "Hey, you can't go up there!"

She stopped to ask another student if he knew where Charlie Stewart's room was. Then she followed his directions until she was standing, breathless, in front of Charlie's open door.

Charlie's head was deep in his books, but he looked up when she cleared her throat. "What the hell? Connie? What are you doing here?" he exclaimed.

Several of his dormmates were gathered outside his room, gaping at her. With very few exceptions, girls weren't allowed upstairs, so here was a spectacle worth enjoying.

The combination of the boys gawking at her from the hallway and Charlie's incredulous expression was almost enough to make Connie lose her nerve. But she had learned her lesson: grab the opportunity when it was there for the taking. And she was afraid she wouldn't get another chance.

"I saw Miranda with Kevin Tawil this afternoon," she said, still catching her breath. "They were looking pretty cozy, and I thought maybe, if you two aren't—"

"Dating?" he said helpfully.

"Yes, dating," she said, forcing herself to continue. "Then maybe you'd consider . . ."

Charlie stood up, walked over to the door, and firmly closed it.

"Me." She swallowed hard. "Again. I know I made a lot of mistakes."

Charlie gathered her into his arms and pressed her to his heart. "But I never make them twice," she said and reached up to meet his lips.

The girls were sitting in Giselle's bedroom, waiting for her to come back from New York with the latest installment about her affair.

"And?" said Joan, as soon as Giselle walked in.

Giselle plopped down into a chair and closed her eyes. "And it was perfect. Romantic. We stayed up all night talking."

"You're lying," Joan said.

"We stayed up all night"—Giselle opened one eye and winked—"not talking."

Connie shook her head in disapproval. "The psychoanalyst again."

Giselle yawned. "Divine exhaustion." She noticed Joan's expression and said, "What?"

"He's married," Joan reminded her.

"Not like you and Tommy are married," said Giselle.

"What does that mean?" Joan asked.

Giselle paraphrased her lover's most frequent complaint. "They don't speak the same language."

"Spelled S-E-X," Connie said snidely.

"Does he pay you?" Betty's voice surprised them all. She must have been standing in the doorway, listening to the discussion. "For sex. At the rate you're going, you could make a fortune. Everyone thinks so, right, Joan? Do you know what they say?"

Giselle ignored Betty and turned instead to Joan. "Is it too late for brunch?" she said, stripping off her rumpled skirt.

This was one conversation she did not want to have, not now, and especially not with Betty. She had fretted all the way from New York to Boston about what to do: tell Betty that Spencer was cheating on her or keep quiet and hope that Betty never found out? She could easily imagine Betty not believing her, calling her a liar or worse.

Betty pointed at finger at Giselle, playing both prosecuting attorney and judge. "They say you're a filthy whore, and pretty soon, once you've been sampled . . ."

Giselle grabbed a clean shirt and tried to block out the rage in Betty's voice. "Shall we go into the city or stay local?" she asked Joan.

"They'll toss you aside," Betty said, starting to sound like a biblical prophet of doom.

Giselle pulled on a skirt and zipped it up. "Local it is."

"Like a used rag," Betty thundered.

"Okay, Betty," Joan shouted, speaking for all of them. "That's enough!"

But Betty was not to be stopped. "Come to think of it, the men you loved most didn't want you at all. Your father, for example."

"Meet you downstairs," Giselle said, picking up her sweater.

The girls were mesmerized by Betty's performance, which was both terrifying and horribly compelling. It was slowly dawning on them that she was completely out of control.

"Professor Dunbar," Betty said. "Everyone knows you wait outside his house."

"Come on, let's go," Joan said, grabbing Giselle's hand.

"It must be torture, running after a man who can't stand the sight of you."

Giselle suddenly understood that she didn't have to make the decision about whether to tell Betty about Spencer. Betty knew. She was talking about herself, about what she was going through with Spencer, as she much as she was talking about Giselle.

"A man who's in love with someone else," Betty said, her voice dropping.

Betty's eyes welled up with tears, and Giselle began to cry, too. She thought of the pain of his betrayal, made all the more vivid seeing Spencer with his mistress.

"Who hates you," Betty said, weeping. "He hates you."

Giselle put her arms around Betty and cradled her as she would a child.

"So much, and it hurts," Betty whispered, sounding like a sad little child.

"I know. I know, honey. It's okay," said Giselle, for lack of any words that could possibly comfort her friend.

"Make it stop," Betty sobbed. "Stop hurting.

He doesn't want me. Spencer doesn't want me."

"Shhh, it's okay," Giselle said, over and over again. "Everything's going to be okay."

Dr. Carr disliked being in the minority. This afternoon, she was an unhappy minority of one, presiding over Katherine Watson's end-of-year review. The alumnae, no doubt incited by Harriet Warren, had a list of grievances long enough to assure themselves that Katherine should not be rehired. Mrs. Warren led the ladies into battle with an opening volley that was meant to surprise the enemy with its subtlety.

"It's unfair to her," Mrs. Warren said, her eyes shining with feigned compassion for Katherine. "She can't be happy."

"Let's not forget the outburst, Jocelyn," said Dorothea Linville, who had learned of Katherine's angry lecture on art and advertising from Lucinda Warren over tea at the Copley Plaza. She had hung on every word of Lucinda's story, so distracted by the details that her tea had grown cold and her watercress sandwich become too soggy to eat.

"She's right," chimed in Ruth Vaughn, who had likewise heard about the incident from Lucinda. "And only six weeks ago."

Dr. Carr's face showed no emotion other than

polite interest as she turned to the department chairman and said, "Dr. Staunton, have you shown the alumnae the statistics?"

Dr. Staunton opened a file folder and handed each of the women a neatly typed up report. He summarized the information for them. "Enrollment for her class next year is the highest the art department's ever had." He sighed, as if wishing he could report otherwise, then repeated himself for emphasis: "Ever."

Dorothea grimaced. As a math major, she respected the integrity of numbers. "She has to promise to turn in lesson plans," she said grudgingly.

"In advance," said Ruth.

"Absolutely, Ruth," Dorothea agreed. "In advance, and they'll need to be approved."

"She'll never agree," said Lucinda, who considered herself the authority on Katherine Watson, because Betty kept her so well-informed.

"She will agree if it's policy," said Dr. Staunton.

Dr. Carr decided it was time to conclude the discussion. "By a show of hands, how many in favor of Katherine Watson coming back next term?" she said, looking around the room. "How many opposed?"

Katherine threw her bike down on his lawn and rushed up the walk to his house. She knocked hard on the door and got no response. He had told her that he kept a key hidden in a flowerpot, and she should feel free to use it, so she found the key and unlocked the door.

She could hear the downstairs shower running. She hurried into the bathroom, threw back the curtain, and screamed, "Surprise!"

The surprise was on her. She shrieked and jumped away from the shower stall. A short, chubby man—a man who was most certainly not Bill—was standing stark naked in front of her.

"Hi," he said, reaching for his glasses.

"Stop right there," Katherine said. She threw him a towel. "Who are you?"

The man grinned, wrapped the towel around himself, and put on his glasses. His grin broadened. "Stanley Sher. I'm an old friend of Bill's," he said. "We were in the Thirty-seventh together. You must be Katherine. He told me you were a looker, but—" He whistled loudly.

"Yeah, well, don't let me interrupt you," Katherine said, embarrassed by her intrusion.

She was still feeling more than a little embarrassed ten minutes later when Stan appeared, fully clothed, in the living room. He was carrying two open bottles of beer, one of which he handed to her.

"You were in the war together?" Katherine said, feeling uncharacteristically shy.

Stan nodded and made himself comfortable on the couch. "Yup. Now he's some fancy teacher, and I'm in air-conditioning. Forget the A-bomb. Freon is going to change the good old U.S. of A. I'm based in El Paso."

Katherine took a sip of beer and relaxed. Stan seemed like a nice fellow, and he obviously had a special bond with Bill because they had been war buddies. "It's a long way from San Remo," she said, recalling Bill's stories.

Stan looked puzzled. "Is that in California?"

"Italy," said Katherine. "Where you and Bill were stationed during the war."

"Italy?" Stan laughed as he stretched out his legs. "Who's been pulling your long leg? We were stationed at the Army Language Institute on Long Island for the whole shmagegie. Closest we ever got to Italy was the baked ziti at Mamma Leone's Restaurant in Midtown Manhattan. Matter of fact, I don't think Bill's ever been to Europe. I sure as hell haven't."

Katherine was waiting for Bill on the porch swing when he got home.

"Katherine!" Bill exclaimed as he bent to kiss the top of her head.

Katherine moved away from him. "I met Stanley."

Bill sat down next to her. "You've been inside?"

"Hell of a nice guy. What a talker."

He nodded. "We go back a long way."

"All the way to Long Island." She stood up. "Secret's out. You can quit lying now."

"It's not a lie."

"What is it?" She had been storing up her anger and hurt, wondering how he would explain the elaborate fabrications and untruths.

"It's a story. I had the uniform. I spoke the language. People assumed things, and I didn't correct them. I guess I should have."

"I guess so."

Her sarcasm ignited his anger. "I don't need to justify anything. I did my part. You want to get mad that I was training officers here so they could fight there, go ahead."

"No, don't do that." His rationalizations only made her angrier. "Don't twist things. You lied. That's why I'm mad."

"Do you think you would have looked twice if you knew I was stateside? Women like you need heroes. You're a sucker for war stories, remember? You're not interested in truth. Truth is—"

"Irrelevant, obviously. So what else was a lie?" she demanded. She stood up, barely able to restrain herself from leaving right then without listening to the rest of his explanation. She wanted him somehow to make it all right, to make her understand why he hadn't been straight with her.

"It took thirty-six years for me to screw myself up. Give me a little time to straighten things out, okay?"

"Why couldn't you have been honest?" she said, so sad that she was past crying.

"Jesus, you don't make it easy! You came with such high expectations that I couldn't be honest."

"No, you couldn't be."

"Not just me, Katherine. Joan let you down, too, didn't she?"

"That's a cheap shot," she said, although she knew he was right, and she hated him for that.

"But it's true. You wanted honesty. So here it comes, sister, like it or not."

She started down the sidewalk, determined not to look back. "I'm leaving. I only stayed to tell you—"

"I know, that I'm a liar. But look in the mirror, sweetheart. How different are we? You didn't come to Wellesley to help people find their way. You came to Wellesley to help people find yours."

Mrs. Warren had spent hours looking for her daughter. The last place she had expected to find her was the library, bent over her books, when her marriage was in tatters, and she should have been patching things up with Spencer.

"There you are!" she exclaimed, her strident voice breaking the hush in the room.

Betty looked up, as did the other girls seated nearby. One of them put a warning finger to her lips, and said, "Shh."

Mrs. Warren lowered her voice. "I'm not accustomed to chasing you down!" she whispered.

Ignoring her, Betty lowered her head and went back to taking notes for her paper on the *Mona Lisa*.

"Look at me, Elizabeth," Mrs. Warren said indignantly, still trying to speak in a whisper. "I'm addressing you."

Old habits died hard. Betty was accustomed to obeying when her mother demanded her attention. She reluctantly raised her eyes to meet another pair so similar to her own.

"I've spoken with Mrs. Jones," said Mrs. Warren. "We've agreed there will be no divorce."

Betty stared wide-eyed at her mother for several moments, feeling torn between laughter and tears by her mother's pronouncement. *How dared she!* And yet, why was she surprised? Lucinda Warren ruled her own little universe; she issued edicts and her subjects obeyed her commands.

Betty couldn't think of anything to say, except to tell her mother to go away and leave her alone. And nobody gave orders to Lucinda Warren. Such a thing was unthinkable. Betty picked up her pen and feigned fascination with Leonardo da Vinci and the *Mona Lisa*.

Mrs. Warren sighed. She wasn't without compassion for her daughter. She could give a semester-long course on the difficulties of marriage. "There's always a period of adjustment for every couple," she said, softening her tone. "Why should you and Spencer be any different?"

At another time in her life, Betty would have put down her books, followed her mother out of the library, and allowed herself to be seduced into submission. But something had changed in her. She had arrived at a place of resolve from which she would not return. The journey had been tortuous, and she knew she faced many more difficulties, but there was no going back to unthinking obedience to her mother, to blind acceptance of her mother's narrow-minded beliefs. Most of all, there was no going back to Spencer.

She picked up the book in front of her and turned it around to show her mother the picture of the *Mona Lisa*. "What do you see, Mother?" she asked quietly.

"I assured her you would try," said Mrs. Warren, not even bothering to glance at the book. "For a year."

Betty almost laughed. In her mother's mind she was still the little girl who had gone against her will to dance class, because her mother had promised the teacher that she would participate.

"The most famous painting in the world?" Betty said, offering the obvious answer.

"Spencer will try, as well," said her mother, continuing on her own mental track. "According to Mrs. Jones, he's been very upset. You should give him a call."

"The most famous smile?" said Betty. "Do you think she's happy, Mother?"

Her mother's face was set in a rigid mask that anyone but Betty might have mistaken for a smile. "The important thing is that you haven't told anyone about this, have you?"

Betty remained obdurately silent. She felt as if she were battling for the right to have her own life, independent of her mother and her husband and the world they embraced.

"Elizabeth?" Her mother prompted her.

"She's beautiful, don't you think?" said Betty, pushed to breaking point. Her voice rising shrilly with each syllable, she said, "And she comes from good pedigree, so does it really matter why she's smiling?"

"Keep your voice down, young lady," her mother warned.

"I didn't used to think so, but I was wrong," Betty said, tears pooling in her eyes. "Sometimes there's more than what appears, Mother. Sometimes you have to look a little harder."

Mrs. Warren glanced around, mortified at the thought that people could hear them. "Don't wash your dirty laundry in public," she hissed.

"And care a little less what other people think," Betty said. She had learned what she could for now from the *Mona Lisa*'s lesson. Slamming shut the book, she grabbed her papers and marched out of the room.

Her mother stood alone, too stunned to move. Betty had always been such a good girl. Suddenly, everything had changed. She had become angry and rebellious, nasty and unpredictable. She was behaving like a crazy person. She was behaving like Katherine Watson.

Katherine took the letter out of her faculty mailbox and saw that the return address read OFFICE OF THE PRESIDENT, WELLESLEY COLLEGE. She took a deep breath before she tore open the envelope. Rumors had been flying all week about which of the nontenured professors would be asked to return. Katherine tried not to pay attention to the gossip. She had heard that her class was oversubscribed for the fall, and she hoped and assumed that would work in her favor.

She unfolded the paper and began to read the typewritten letter, signed by President Carr:

> Dear Miss Watson,
>
> It is with great pleasure that we invite you to return as an instructor in the art history department for the 1954/55 academic year.

She stifled an exultant whoop and wished Bill was right there to share her excitement. Wondering whether the question of her salary had been addressed, she read on.

> We do wish to make clear, however, that this invitation is conditional upon the following:
>
> 1. You will teach only the syllabus as outlined by the department chair.
> 2. All lesson plans must be submitted at the beginning of every term for approval and revision.
> 3. You shall not provide counsel, beyond your own subject, for any student, at any time.
> 4. You will abide by our standard morals

clause stating that you will agree to maintain a strictly professional relationship with all members of the faculty.

Assuming you accept the above conditions, we look forward to your becoming a part of our Wellesley traditions.

Sincerely,
Jocelyn Carr
President
Wellesley College

If she hadn't known better, she might have thought it was a joke concocted by someone with a macabre sense of humor. Surely, Dr. Carr and Dr. Staunton could not believe that she would ever accept such insulting conditions. They demeaned her professionalism, made her sound like a dangerous character who had to be kept in check. If they hadn't wanted to rehire her, they should have said so straight out, rather than offer her the position with so many strings attached that she would risk being strangled with each step she took.

She had wanted and intended to remain at Wellesley. After today's conversation with Bill, she saw her situation in a different light. Now she was prepared to cut the bonds she had begun to develop at the college. She would miss some of the girls, but they were leaving, too. She and Nancy had become unlikely friends, and she would miss sharing her house and her meals. And Bill . . . Ah, well, she supposed they weren't mean to be together, and Dr. Carr had just handed her a gift of a graceful exit.

It had been a day filled with surprises: learning that she had been invited back to teach at Wellesley, stumbling upon Stan in the shower, and finding out that Bill had lied to her about his army experience. When she got home, Katherine discovered one more surprise. Nancy had thrown her a party to celebrate the renewal of her contract. But she had stayed so late at Bill's that she had missed the whole thing.

CONGRATULATIONS! declared the large banner that hung across the living room window. On an end table, she found a card signed by many of the colleagues who had become her friends this past year. The card said: CONGRATULATIONS ON THE NEW JOB!

Katherine followed the sound of the TV into the den and found Nancy watching one of her favorite game shows. "Quite the party. I didn't know."

"It was a surprise," said Nancy, one eye still on the program. She heard the question, quickly came up with the answer. "The pyramids."

"I'm sorry, Bob," said the television announcer to the hapless contestant. "Your time is up. The correct answer is the pyramids."

The show went to a commercial for toothpaste. Nancy turned and said, "Don't worry. What's important is that you'll be back next year. Living here, I hope."

Katherine shrugged, uncommitted. "I haven't even thought about that. They just told me today."

"Well, there's plenty of time. Right now, you should celebrate," Nancy said.

"Good idea!" She had much to celebrate, although not a second year of teaching at Wellesley. On an impulse, Katherine turned off the television set.

"Hey!" Nancy protested.

Katherine pulled her up off the sofa. "Come on, let's get out of here. Get gussied up. Let's go dancing. Life isn't about *What's My Line?*"

Nancy switched the TV back on. "It's *Strike It Rich* silly. And it's after eight o'clock on a school night."

"So what?"

"So I don't want to go," Nancy said, settling back into the cushions. "I'm happy here."

The stark truth of her statement hit Katherine with the force of a sudden summer thunderstorm. Nancy was completely happy spending her life on the couch, watching TV. Perhaps President Carr's letter was fate's way of telling Katherine that it was time to move on.

"Shh, the program's back on," Nancy said, her gaze riveted to the television. She pointed to the contestant. "He's handsome, right?"

Katherine nodded, and her eyes unexpectedly filled with tears. Nancy had been a good friend to her right from the start. Despite their different backgrounds and attitudes, and the fact that she disapproved of Katherine's relationship with Bill, she was still generous and openhearted with Katherine.

"Watch with me?" Nancy asked.

Katherine sat down next to her on the sofa. Bill's parting shot replayed itself in her mind: *You didn't come to Wellesley to help people find their way. You came to Wellesley to help people find yours.* Well, he might not be altogether wrong. Her mother had called her pigheaded, a quality that had served her well over the years. But as much as she hated to admit it, her single-minded stubbornness sometimes prevented her from recognizing other people's realities.

Nancy's choices weren't right for Katherine, but Nancy was satisfied with the circumstances she had carved out for herself. And nothing was set in stone, except for a piece of sculpture that had withstood the erosion of time. It wasn't up to Katherine to chip away at Nancy's fears and defenses. The best she could do was totally accept her for who she was.

"For two thousand dollars, Bob," the game show host was saying, "what is the name of this popular big band tune?"

" 'You Made Me Love You!' " Katherine and Nancy shouted in unison.

Life was complicated. That was what made it so interesting. Yet sometimes the simplest pleasures were the most rewarding. And sometimes the most obvious questions were the ones that were hardest to answer.

Katherine stood in front of the lecture hall, about to teach her final class. Eight months had passed since she had met this group of girls, learned their names, discovered their strengths and weaknesses. Their time together had passed so quickly. It was hard to believe she would never see them again like this, their faces eagerly turned toward hers, connected by the particular magic that sometimes occurs between teacher and students.

She turned on the slide projector for the last time this year; the image of the *Mona Lisa* appeared on the wall. She said, "In 1503, Francesco del Giocondo asked Leonardo da Vinci to paint his new wife, Lisa. She had just given birth to their first son. Is that why she's smiling? Some scholars have argued recently that this isn't Lisa at all. Rather, that it is a self-portrait of da Vinci's female side. Hence, the smile. It's the most famous painting in the world."

She looked out at them and saw how intently they were listening. They didn't know it, but their willingness to consider her ideas was their graduation gift to her. She was grateful beyond measure for it.

She smiled and said, "You know what? I don't like it. I've never liked it. I never understood what everybody is so excited about. I like other da Vincis. I love *The Last Supper*. But this one doesn't appeal to me."

She pointed to the screen. "Art doesn't happen up there." She pointed to her head, then put her hand on her heart. "Art happens in here—and here. Just because something is considered classic doesn't mean you are required to love it. Its beauty lies with the individual."

She glanced at her watch. Her time was almost up. Soon this group of girls would go out into the world. She could only hope that something she had said this past year would make a difference in how they viewed the world.

"Don't let anyone define your truth," she said. "The answers are inside all of you magnificent, strong-minded women."

She turned off the projector and motioned to Connie to turn on the lights. The girls seemed to be smiling at one another, as if they had some wonderful secret. Katherine looked around the room one last time, then left for her office.

Later, Katherine opened the door to her office and was about to set down her things when something caught the corner of her eye—a small painting of van Gogh's *Sunflowers*. And another, sitting by her desk. She heard a noise behind her, and turning, she saw that the girls had followed her, giggling openly now.

Connie handed Katherine a small package. Inside was another copy of van Gogh's *Sunflowers,* from a paint-by-numbers kit, but this rendering was free-form, the colors vibrant, the paint splashed haphazardly outside the lines. Van Gogh as painted by Pollock. *Love, Connie,* said the message on the other side.

One by one, the girls came forward with their versions of the masterpieces they had discussed during the year. The pictures were rendered with a child's playful imagination and freedom, before the adult constraints of "right" and "wrong" were imposed.

"Thank you," said Katherine. "I will carry your faces with me for a lifetime."

"It was Joan's idea," said Connie.

"How else will you remember us?" said Joan, as if Katherine could ever forget them.

* * *

There was one last Wellesley tradition for Katherine to enjoy: a reception in honor of the seniors, their families, and the faculty held in the Tower Courtyard on the afternoon before graduation day. No need for tents this year: the sun was shining, the sky as blue as Lake Waban—picture-perfect weather to celebrate the picture-perfect girls of Wellesley College.

A harried photographer and his assistant were trying to organize the faculty, seniors, and Alumnae Association officers to pose for a class picture.

"Katherine! Over here!" Nancy called to her above the din of voices.

Katherine took her place between Nancy and Violet Albini. Betty and Giselle hurried over to join the group.

"Elizabeth? I don't see Spencer," said Betty's mother, who was standing in the same row as Katherine.

"Neither do I. Excuse me, Mother," Betty said, turning to Katherine. "Miss Watson, can you help me get in touch with that friend of yours in Greenwich Village?"

"What do you need in Greenwich Village?" Mrs. Warren asked nervously.

"An apartment," Betty said. "Mother, you remember Giselle Levy, that New York— What was it you called her? Oh, yes. A New York kike."

Giselle made a mock curtsey. *Kike.* . . . Leave it to Betty's mother to label her with such a vicious racial slur.

"Well, she and I are going to be roommates," Betty said. "I filed for divorce this morning, and since we know I'm not welcome at your house . . ."

Her mother stared at her. For perhaps the first time in her life, Lucinda Warren was completely at a loss for words.

A waiter passed by with a tray of champagne. Betty grabbed a glass and swallowed the contents in one gulp.

"What are you doing?" asked her horrified mother.

Betty smiled happily. "I don't know. For the first time ever, I don't know." She turned to Giselle. "Ready?"

"You bet." Giselle nodded.

"Greenwich Village?" said Katherine.

"For a while, yes. Then, who knows? Maybe law school. Maybe even Yale. What would you think about me becoming a lawyer?" asked Betty.

Katherine's smile matched Betty's. "I wouldn't want to come up against you in any court."

"I'll never forget you," Betty said, blinking back tears.

"Same here," said Katherine.

"Maybe I can drop in on one of your classes next year, to keep you on your toes. You will be here, Miss Watson, won't you?"

Then, surprising Katherine and herself, she threw her arms around her teacher and hugged her. There was so much she wanted to say: apologies, explanations, questions she was dying to ask. But people were waiting, and now was not the right time. The important thing, Betty told herself, was that she could come back and visit, make friends with Miss Watson, instead of using her for target practice. She hoped Miss Watson could forgive her for her many unkind remarks, most especially for the infamous editorial in which she had singled Miss Watson out as the enemy.

Katherine hadn't wanted to ruin such a perfect afternoon by announcing that she wasn't coming back, so she had merely smiled in response to Betty's question. They would have time enough to find out in the fall, once they were ensconced in their new postcollege lives. Then she changed her mind. Her father had walked out on her without even a good-bye, and she would never stop wondering why. She had formed a relationship with these girls. She had struggled with them, earned their trust, taught them something, she hoped, and learned a lot in return. She owed them some explanation, a gesture of her love and respect.

It took a while to figure out what she wanted to say, and then she realized she had different messages for each of the girls. But her letter to Betty, with whom she had had the most complicated relationship, best summed up her feelings:

My dear Betty,

I am writing to you and everyone in the class to let you know that I feel I can no longer continue to teach at Wellesley. I am very sorry for it. I have found my time here enormously fulfilling, but for my own sake, I have to get out into the world and discover fresh inspiration. I came to Wellesley because I wanted to make a difference. If I can't do that, I don't know what my purpose is, so I must leave.

There are times in our lives when events overwhelm us, times when the demands of other people, their needs, can be crushing. I now believe I saw in you a person in the grip of such a struggle, desperately wanting to be free. I wish you joy in the rest of your life. You—all of you—are magnificent, strong young women. You have inspired me. I have learned from you every bit as much as I've taught you. Perhaps out of our troubles, there comes a gift: that you, particularly you, will live in my memory always.

I send you love,

Katherine Watson

Chapter Ten

Betty wrote her final editorial for *The Daily Wellesley* with tears streaming down her cheeks. She had been wondering for days what she would say, how she could summarize her experiences at Wellesley and send a message to her readers that was truthful, yet not bitter. She had gone through several drafts of the first paragraph, hated the inadequacy of her words, ripped the sheets from her typewriter, and balled them up into the wastepaper basket.

Finally, at the last possible moment before the paper had to be put to bed, she picked up her mail and found the letter from Katherine. She read through it once, hardly remembering to breathe, reread it, then rushed over to the newspaper office, writing the editorial in her head as she bicycled across the campus.

The words tumbled out as if they had been stored in her brain all along, a story waiting to be told:

> At first she was just a nuisance. We'd heard about bohemians before, but we'd never actually met one. It was obvious in the beginning that she didn't belong. But she was the only one who didn't know it. Katherine Watson came to Wellesley because she wanted to make a difference.
>
> But to change for others is to lie to yourself. As a graduating senior, I dedicate this, my last editorial, to Katherine Watson, a woman who changed my life and refused to compromise her own. Most of you will never know her. She was no hero, nor mentor, nor even a friend. She was simply my teacher, who compelled me to see the world with new eyes, and who compelled herself to live by example.

Betty stopped and stared at the opposite wall, seeing there the slides Katherine had shown them: of Soutine's *Carcass* and Jackson Pollock's paint-spattered canvases, of Katherine's thin, cancer-ridden mother just before she died and the *Mona Lisa*. Then her fingers flew back to the typewriter keys.

By the time you read this, she'll be sailing to Europe, where I know she'll find new artists to discover, new walls to break down, and new ideas to replace them with. I've heard her called a quitter for leaving. An aimless wanderer. But remember, not all who wander are aimless. Especially not those who seek truth beyond tradition, beyond definition, beyond the image.

I'll never forget you.

As Betty concluded, she wished she had had the chance to say those words aloud to Katherine.

She stood up, walked around the room once, returned to her chair, and reread the editorial. It was the best piece she had ever written.

Katherine's mind was rushing with thoughts. As she looked out the window of the taxi, her excitement about the future was tempered by her sadness about the life she was leaving behind.

Suddely, Katherine caught a glimpse through the open window of a girl in a grudation cap and gown pedaling a bike furiously. Leaning forward, she realized that the hair flying every which way and arms waving madly belonged to Betty. Katherine saw that Joan, Connie,

Giselle, and the others were following behind on their bikes, all of them in caps and gowns as well, pumping their legs frantically to draw abreast of the taxi. They were calling her name, shouting, "Thank you, Miss Watson! Thank you! We'll never forget you, Miss Watson! Good luck!"

Katherine had said her good-byes to Nancy, Violet, and the other faculty members who had become her friends. She had even, at the last minute, called Bill, half hoping he wouldn't be home. She wasn't sure what she wanted to say or how he would respond. They hadn't spoken since that afternoon at his house, when things had ended so badly, and she had made a point of avoiding him on campus. But when he picked up the phone and said hello, she smiled with relief. She could tell that he was pleased to hear from her.

Friends? Lovers? The label didn't matter. They had shared wonderful conversations, laughter, moments of fun, more intimate moments fed by deep caring, perhaps even love. She would miss him, but their relationship wasn't reason enough to stay at Wellesley. They had promised to keep in touch, although she knew she wouldn't, not out of spite, but because it was time to move on, to take down the collage in her office and create a new design for her life. Saying good-bye to Bill felt bittersweet, but she tried to let him know that she wasn't leaving Wellesley because she was running away from him. At least she hoped she wasn't.

She hadn't said a proper good-bye to her students, because she couldn't trust herself to face them without crying. Back home in Los Angeles, she had liked and respected many of her students at Oakland Teachers College. But none of them had gotten under her skin, challenged her, stretched her horizons, tested her patience, won her affection and admiration as these Wellesley girls had. If she ever were blessed to have a daughter, she hoped her child might develop some of their same qualities and traits.

She had wept, reading Betty's last newspaper article, stunned to realize how deeply this group had affected her. She had imagined herself, knowing what she did now, starting over with them. But she was leaving, and so were they. She had done her best, and in the end, she had made a difference. She had always thought she was her own worst critic, until she met Betty, and ultimately she had earned even Betty's respect.

She stuck her arm out the window, almost reaching Betty's outstretched hand. The cab driver yelped, "Hey! What's going on?" He swerved to avoid having an accident as a small battalion of bicycles surrounded the taxi from the rear.

Katherine blew kisses and waved as the girls escorted her off campus. Her own personal honor guard. She couldn't have dreamed of a better sendoff.

From time to time Katherine's name would come up among the girls whom she had taught that year. Joan, Betty, and the others would cling to the rumors and savor them, like a beautiful painting they could admire from afar. They liked to think she was out there, still breaking down new walls and forming new ideas, just as they were, in the tumultuous times that signaled the end of the complacent fifties.

The core group of them stayed in touch, getting together for lunch or drinks or dinner whenever they could find the time. Sometimes the gap between their reunions was a few months, sometimes longer than that. Betty was often too busy with her law practice; one or another of Connie's three children always seemed to be sick; Tommy's company sent him to Japan for a year to run its overseas division, and Joan came back speaking Japanese.

Greenwich Village was always their favorite meeting place. They were loyal to one particular restaurant, an unpretentious French place around the corner from the tiny brownstone apartment where Betty and Giselle lived right after graduation.

Giselle had summoned them this time, luring them in with a new Miss Watson sighting. She was already seated at their corner table with Joan and Giselle when Betty bolted out of a taxi and rushed into the restaurant.

"We did say one o'clock," Joan reminded her. Betty was always running late, and Joan had to get back to Larchmont in time to pick up the kids from school.

"How are you feeling?" Betty asked Connie.

Connie laughed and pointed to her belly. "I'm eight and a half months pregnant, and I always deliver early. You guess."

"Well, you look fantastic," Giselle said to Betty.

Betty blew her a kiss and performed a quick pirouette to show off her new, very expensive suit, which she had bought to celebrate her latest court victory.

"All right, where is it?" she demanded of Giselle.

"She wouldn't show us until you got here," said Connie, sounding exasperated.

"This better be worth it," said Joan.

Giselle pulled out of her bag a copy of *Paris Match* magazine, which she had picked up in France while there to cover the spring fashion shows for *Vogue,* where she was an editor. "It's from May. The Cannes Film Festival."

She turned to a picture of actor William Holden, arm in arm with a tall, elegantly dressed woman whose face was half shielded by her oversize hat. The girls scrutinized the photograph as carefully as if they were examining a newly acquisitioned painting at the Metropolitan Museum of Art.

"It looks like her," Joan said.

"It's her," Giselle insisted. "I know it."

Betty shook her head. "You can't tell."

"It *is* her," said Connie. "Oh, my God! She's dating William Holden."

"I heard she's living in Florence," said Joan, who knew people in the art world.

"An old friend comes to town, spur of the moment, invites her to the south of France," said Giselle, dreamily spinning out the story.

On her first trip to Paris, she had made a pilgrimage to the Louvre to see the *Mona Lisa*. She had recalled Miss Watson's comments about the subject's unresolved identity, but unlike Miss Watson she loved the portrait with its enigmatic smile.

"She looks fantastic. I always thought she was so much older. Now the difference between us is hardly anything," Connie said.

Joan sighed. "I'd love to see her again, have a chance to chat about things."

"Me, too. Just once, to catch up. Let me see that again," said Betty, grabbing the magazine. "I think you're right. It is Miss Watson."

"Of course, it's Miss Watson. Perfect, right?" said Giselle.

Four heads nodded in unison. Four friends, no longer girls, but women now, heading into still uncharted territories. For one special year, a special woman had touched their lives. She had been the right teacher at the right time. A perfect fit.

As perfect—and mysterious—as the Mona Lisa smile.